Praise for Bianca D'Arc's *Prince of Spies*

5 Angels & Recommended Read! "Bianca D'Arc continues to awe me with her Dragon Knights series. Each is unique, and yet a strong plot flows through making you want more, more, more.... Her characters are innocent and carnal at the same time, and I am impressed that she has been able to continue this throughout the series...I have to give Prince of Spies, the fourth in a fantastic series, a Recommended Read rating."

~ *Serena, Fallen Angel Reviews*

5 Hearts "I think that Prince of Spies is the best one of the series so far. I really liked Nico, he is his own man and is quite ruthless when he needs to be. Riki has had a hard life, but manages to come across as a strong person who will survive. The sex between the two is definitely out of this world, passionate and honest, it really adds to the story. ...I believe that you could read this one as a stand alone, but once you do you will want to race out and buy the other three from the series. Prince of Spies is a fantastic story that shouldn't be missed."

~ *Julia, The Romance Studio*

5 Klovers "Prince of Spies, takes the series to a whole new level with the introduction of some exciting and very mysterious new characters."

~ *Jennifer, CK²S Kwips and Kritiques*

5 Cups: "...a fantastic read. Ms. D'Arc creates characters that inspire dreams of love and romance in the most jaded reader. Her world building skills are absolutely the best... Anyone who likes dragons and magic should scoop up this book and read it as soon as possible."

~ *Susan, Coffee Time Romance*

5 Kisses "...an erotic tale of seduction and secrets. With each tale in the Dragon Knights series, Bianca D'Arc slowly reveals more about the upcoming battle... I thoroughly enjoyed the play between Nico and Riki. Each time they share passion, it's hotter than the last, culminating in a scene that will blow you away."

~ *Tara Renee, Two Lips Reviews*

"I recommend PRINCE OF SPIES wholeheartedly. Imaginative, full of interesting twists and turns, this book and the others are simply not to be missed."

~ *Lori Ann, Romance Reviews Today Erotic*

Prince of Spies

Bianca D'Arc

A Samhain Publishing, Ltd. publication.

Samhain Publishing, Ltd.
512 Forest Lake Drive
Warner Robins, GA 31093
www.samhainpublishing.com

Print ISBN: 1-59998-425-3
Digital ISBN: 1-59998-331-1

Editing by Jessica Bimberg
Cover by Scott Carpenter

First Samhain Publishing, Ltd. electronic publication: February 2007
First Samhain Publishing, Ltd. print publication: September 2007

Dedication

With much love and appreciation, to my readers and the friends I've made through this endeavor, especially Megan and Serena, who are always there to chat when I need an ear or an opinion.

To Rosemary of Rosemary's Romance Books in Brisbane, whose dedication to romance books is unmatched in my experience. She's a treasure!

To my editor, Jess, for her patient guidance, and to Sharon, whose insight is always keen and much appreciated. I've learned a great deal from both of you and am glad of your friendship. You ROCK, ladies!

To the folks on my chat group and some of my fellow writers whose enthusiasm really keeps me going, especially Jennifer, Stella Price, Jacki Frank, Rene Lyons, Jennie Andrus, Candice Gilmer, and many others. Without friends, writing can be a very lonely occupation.

And to my moral support system and #1 cheerleaders—my family. You've always told me to reach for my goals and follow my dreams. Thanks for believing in me now, in this radical new adventure.

Prologue

Under cover of darkness, the black dragon slipped across the border into Skithdron, his dark hide blending with the night. Nico truly was the Prince of Spies and he was on a noble quest. The North Witch, Loralie, had intimated that his new queen's missing sister was in Skithdron, but Nico hoped his agents might provide more specific information.

Aside from locating the girl, Nico also had some spying to do on the neighboring king and his troops. Things were not yet settled between the two kingdoms and Nico feared more violence was coming. Such was the way with tyrants.

Nico's brother, King Roland, had routed the tyrannical warlord, Salomar, to the north and now celebrated with his new queen, Alania. It would be up to Nico to gather enough intelligence to defeat the despot to the east, King Lucan.

Mission firmly in mind, Prince Nico landed on the outskirts of the Skithdronian capital city some hours later. He changed swiftly and secretly from dragon to human form. His contact would meet him shortly. Hopefully he'd have the information Nico needed—or at least another piece to the puzzle that was slowly taking shape.

Nico was eager, but not stupid. He'd searched the ground from above while still cloaked in the stealthy darkness of his dragon shape. The immediate area of the pre-arranged meet seemed clear, but Nico approached cautiously, eyes wary for any sign of trouble.

When it came, however, trouble still caught him by surprise. A troop of Skithdronian royal guards surrounded him before he could react. He dared not change to dragon form in front of so many witnesses. Odds were he couldn't kill them all before escaping, and the secret of the royal black dragons was too precious to reveal so clumsily. He would hold that in reserve. For now, Nico allowed himself to be shackled and led away toward the enemy king's palace. He wanted to get a look inside anyway, though he would have chosen another method had it been left up to him. Still, this would get him in. Once inside, he had little doubt he would be able to free himself. There wasn't a chain or shackle made that could hold a black dragon.

With an almost jaunty stride, Nico went to face whatever waited. There was more at stake in this game than just his own personal safety. No, the security of Draconia itself was at stake, and the safety of his land and people was more important than anything.

Chapter One

King Lucan's guards shoved Nico into the ornate room. They had manhandled him from the street to the guardhouse, to the dungeon and now here, to King Lucan's private chambers. Nico knew being brought so quickly before the reclusive king of Skithdron meant one of his network of spies had either been compromised or sold out. Nico vowed to find out which at the earliest opportunity and mete out any punishment that might be necessary. Selling out the Royal Spymaster of Draconia was grounds for death and it would come, swift and certain, if such was the case.

Nico searched the room as the guards shoved him roughly inside. He couldn't control the jolt of surprise when he caught sight of the poor creature chained at the foot of Lucan's large bed. It was a girl clothed in rags, with deep, dark circles under eerily familiar, luminous green eyes. She was mere skin and bones, clinging desperately to life, and while he couldn't be absolutely certain of her identity, Nico began to suspect.

"Do you like my little witch?" Lucan asked from a shadowed corner of the grand room. Nico cursed inwardly, realizing he'd gazed too long at the bedraggled waif, betraying his interest. "You can look," Lucan moved into the light wagging one bony finger at him, "but don't touch."

Nico shifted his gaze to the king and was shocked by what he saw. Always an ascetic man, King Lucan seemed almost snake-like now, with dark, scaly patches on the small amount of skin Nico could see. Lucan wore ornate robes of state that covered most of his body, hanging off his thin form as he paced and continued to rant.

"The witch's power is lost if she's not virgin."

Nico tried not to choke on his startled laughter. If Lucan truly believed such drivel, he was crazier than they'd thought!

But then, perhaps belief in that little lie was the only thing saving the girl from even worse treatment. Rape was not above Lucan. Nico's spy network kept him well informed about Lucan's perverted entertainments. It was well-known he found pleasure in ghastly forms of torture all civilized lands had long banned.

Nico tried not to look too interested in the girl but her desperate green eyes drew him. She was no doubt suffering, chained and ill-treated by the despot who was only steps away from utter madness.

"I hear your King Roland fornicates with dragons. There are even rumors he drinks their blood, thereby gaining some of their power." Lucan's crazy eyes sidled along Nico's form, making his skin itch. That cinched it. This bastard was completely insane and poorly informed, if he wasn't just playing some game. Perhaps Nico could use it to his advantage.

"Is that what you've done, Lucan? Are you fucking skiths now and drinking their blood?"

In a flash, Lucan went from mild questioner to irate combatant. His eyes...changed. They went from human brown to slitted gold as he hissed.

"I ask the questions! Not you! Not you!"

Lucan seemed to consciously reign in his temper, breathing in deep, hissing breaths as he turned away. Nico couldn't help watching the girl while Lucan's back was turned. There was something about her that drew him. She was in bad shape, her hair lank and an indeterminate, unhealthy color. Her skin was sallow, pale beyond the norm, and covered with little burns, as if she had been tortured with skith venom.

Cringing inwardly, Nico realized it was more than likely the poor creature had indeed suffered such inhuman torture. He would put nothing past Lucan.

Only her eyes seemed to reflect the life still clinging to her pathetically thin body. Malnourished and weak, she had heavy chains manacling both hands and feet. Her sack of a dress was stained and burned in several places—a byproduct of skith venom torture, no doubt.

The rising fire in him warned of slipping control. His dragon side wanted nothing more than to flame everyone in the room, free the girl, and whisk her off somewhere to get cleaned up and eat her fill. He wanted to take care of her and make it so no one would ever hurt her again. He wanted to hold her in his arms and stroke her delicate shoulders, protecting her from all harm.

It was a startling thought.

Nico was not normally a sentimental man. It was hard to hold on to the softer emotions in his line of work. As Spymaster to the king of Draconia, he'd seen all too often how some people would sell out their own mothers for the right amount of coin. He'd been disillusioned early in his chosen profession, and the more tender emotions hadn't plagued him since.

Until now.

Until this poor little waif with the emerald green eyes.

Lucan turned back to him, seemingly under control once more. His eyes had reverted to human brown, but there was a wild sparkle in them that told Nico this man was far from in control of whatever evil modifications he'd made to his being.

"Let's try this again. What are you doing in my land?"

Nico eyed the unstable king defiantly. "Sightseeing."

Lucan nodded over at one of his burly guards and a moment later, the man's fist was planted deep in Nico's gut. It took a lot to injure someone of his gifts, but that had definitely hurt. Nico knew he was in for a long evening.

"You'll have to do better than that. I know you're a spy for the Draconian bastard. In fact," Lucan trailed a sharp, discolored fingernail over Nico's jaw as his guards held him tightly around the upper arms, "I know you're one of the senior agents."

Nico wondered if Lucan wasn't just playing with him. If Lucan truly didn't realize who he was, Nico might yet live through this session. Even better, if Lucan didn't know who he truly was, this was an excellent opportunity to gather firsthand information about the rogue king.

Too bad he couldn't just kill Lucan outright and end their troubles. But Nico knew all too well that getting rid of Lucan now would only cause more problems. First, the skirmishes on the borders had been repelled and an uneasy peace existed, though both sides of the border were poised for an explosion that could come at any time. Second, there was no clear succession in Skithdron. They could remove Lucan only to have someone even worse take the helm.

No, Lucan had to fall in battle, do himself in, or be taken down by his own people. Draconia couldn't be seen to have any part in his demise unless it were by fair means. So that left Nico's hands tied—both literally and figuratively. He had to take whatever Lucan dished out here, this evening, and learn what he could. Only then would Nico make his escape, and he'd take the poor creature with the sad eyes with him.

It went on for hours. Lucan asked questions that were increasingly erratic and Nico refused to answer a single one. Each refusal earned him a blow of some kind and as the night wore on, Lucan produced vials of skith venom to add to the torture. Through it all, the skinny girl watched silently, her expression only showing sympathy when Lucan's back was turned. Nico tried not to look at her, but found himself stealing glances when Lucan couldn't see, using her luminous face to keep him grounded in the here and now as pain threatened to overwhelm him.

Nico learned a great deal about Lucan in those hours, and made some enlightening self-discoveries as well. He learned how much pain he could withstand and just what it might take to break him. Fortunately, it never came to that point. The massive reserves of dragon strength and magic in his soul saw him through the worst of it.

Finally Lucan halted the torture, wiping Nico's blood from his hands onto a clean white towel as Nico dropped to the floor, fading fast. Dimly, he heard Lucan's final words as he swept from the room.

"Heal him, little bitch." Lucan threw the soiled towel at the girl. "And clean up this mess. I can't sleep here with his blood stinking up the place. I'll be back for more in the morning."

The last thing Nico thought as his vision dimmed was that if this was any indication of what the poor waif had been through at Lucan's hands, Nico didn't know how she had survived.

She said nothing as Lucan stalked from the room, though she was grateful for the reprieve. Having him take his perversions to some other room for the night was like a gift. Since Lucan's change, she'd been made to witness all kinds of disgusting acts that were inhuman as well as deadly. Only her healing powers had saved some of Lucan's victims, and some had begged for death. Lucan sometimes obliged, when the whim took him.

She knew he wasn't stable. Any little thing could send him into a rage. When that happened, she often feared for her own life, even though he'd been cautioned not to kill her by the North Witch.

That evil woman was to blame for her current circumstances. The North Witch, Loralie, had told Lucan to keep her close, exposing her healing gift to him. Loralie had changed Lucan into the half-human creature he was now. It was Loralie, too, who cautioned him not to kill the young healer and warned Lucan how rare the healing gift was. She foresaw another healer would not be found again within the borders of Skithdron. Loralie was the reason she was subjected to Lucan's perversions, tortured when the mood struck him and kept chained to his bed.

But oddly, Loralie was also to thank for Lucan leaving her sexually unmolested. The North Witch had told the mad king that the healing magic would be forever lost should anyone breach her maidenhead. The old magic, Loralie claimed, would depart as soon as she was no longer a virgin. For that reason alone, Lucan hadn't raped her. He'd tortured her, played with her flesh, hurt her in ways that didn't bear thinking about, but he hadn't taken her virginity. For that small boon, she supposed she should thank the witch, but she just couldn't bring herself to do it.

The witch was back in the north now, with her master, King Salomar. She'd done the sickening work of merging Lucan with the skiths and gone back to her own king. The girl was left to heal the recurring injuries of a body never meant to hold two such diametrically opposed essences in one space. She figured Lucan would die a slow and agonizing death without her constant healing treatments and almost wished he'd go too far and kill her one day so he would die too.

But somehow she couldn't bring herself to goad him into that final, irrevocable act. Something inside her fought to hang on. Some kernel of hope remained. Hope that somehow she would get a chance at escape or a chance to kill Lucan herself. Either would do.

She struggled to her feet, knowing she would have to clean up first, then see to the fallen warrior. After she gave him her healing energy, she would be too weak to move for several hours. If the room was dirty when Lucan returned, she would pay a heavy price, so she scrubbed the blood away, cleaning in a familiar rhythm. She'd been ordered to do this before. She knew what was expected.

After over an hour of scrubbing, the room was clean and everything put back to rights within the length of her chain tether. Only then did she settle by the fallen man, stroking back locks of long, dark hair from his chiseled face. He would be badly scarred without her help. As it was, she didn't know how much energy she could give him. She was dangerously weak. Lucan kept her that way so she wouldn't try to escape—or if she did manage to escape, she wouldn't be able to get far.

Settling next to the man, she looked to his worst wounds first. She sent little pulses of her energy, rationing it as best she could, to make him as strong as possible before her own energy gave out. He was a brave man. She'd never seen one of Lucan's victims defy the crazy king so long or so well. This foreign warrior impressed her and stirred a womanly interest she'd thought long dead.

After watching Lucan's bed sport over the past months, she never thought she would feel any kind of attraction for a man again. Lucan was brutal. She didn't know if she could trust a man not to turn into a beast like Lucan if she ever gave one the chance. Plus, her virginity was the only thing protecting her. If she lost that, she lost everything—her power, her tenuous position, and most probably her life.

The man groaned as she touched the savage wounds on his torso. Skith venom burns ate away at the skin, causing agony unmatched by anything else. She knew it from painful, firsthand experience. She had skith venom burns all over her body thanks to Lucan. It was one of his ways to remind her of her position and warn her not to cross him.

The warrior's skin was hot and feverish, but her healing gift confirmed he was in prime health aside from the torture he'd just undergone. She didn't understand it, but like her, his normal body temperature seemed to be a bit higher than most other humans she'd treated.

His warmth was comforting as her strength waned. He'd gone from pain-laden unconsciousness to more normal sleep while she sent healing energy to his battered form. At least she'd been able to do that much for him, allowing him to rest easy before the next round with Lucan. The injured man would need whatever she could give. So thinking, she concentrated the last of her remaining strength in one final, powerful burst, sending it to the terrible burns on his face. He had such a strong, handsome face, she thought it a shame to have it scar.

Slipping into oblivion, she settled down at his side, her hand over his heart, her head resting on his shoulder as she unconsciously snuggled closer to his warmth. Just before the darkness claimed her, a stray thought drifted across her mind. She had never been so comfortable in all the years since being stolen from her home. For just this short moment, she was finally at peace.

Chapter Two

Nico woke to the rich scent of woman in his nostrils. Unsure of his surroundings, he immediately noted the soft, female form snuggled at his side. She was thin and shaking with cold, clinging to him for warmth. He opened his eyes and was startled to see the girl there, her elfin face resting against his heart.

Something inside him twinged at the sight. The sleeping dragon inside him woke, possessively pulling the small woman closer as if to never let her go. Nico noticed then the energy flowing between them, from him to her and back again, making them both stronger. Already he could see a bloom of healthy color on her pale cheeks and a new vibrancy to her previously pasty skin.

He took a moment to savor and examine the connection. It was like nothing he'd ever experienced before, but he'd heard of it surely enough. In the ancient texts of his ancestors there were tales of this kind of sharing, and his own brother had mentioned just such a phenomenon when he'd met his new wife. A dragon healer might be able to absorb and reflect the massive power of his dragon half, strengthening them both in the process.

He looked more closely at the beautiful waif in his arms. No wonder he'd been so drawn to her when all other females left him cold. This poor, starved woman was almost certainly his new sister-in-law's twin, though she looked far different from the robust woman his brother had just married. No, this poor creature had been starved and tortured for months, perhaps years, but there was still a marked resemblance to the healthy woman she should be.

There were her eyes for one thing. Nico had been struck by the luminescent green of her eyes right off. Royal green, some in Draconia called the color, since many of royal blood had just that shade, unlike himself. Nico was the rarity among the royal princes, with his tourmaline gaze. Most had the deep emerald of this woman's eyes.

Her hair would probably be a deep, blazing auburn if it were healthy. Even under her pallor and the poor state of her clothing, it shone with reddish highlights, very much like her sister's. She was the same height as well and had similar bone structure, though this poor girl's features stood out much too prominently, her body mere skin and bones.

She stirred in his arms as if she felt his close study and her giant eyes opened into his. Nico caught his breath, knowing this poor girl was the reason he'd come to Skithdron. When he thought his mission utterly failed, she'd come to him as if the Mother of All had brought them together.

And indeed, perhaps She had. Nico had no other explanation for the set of dire circumstances that led him directly to the girl. She blinked and tried to move away but Nico held her firmly, though not harshly, his gaze gently questioning.

"Arikia?" He breathed her name, watching reaction jolt through her. She recognized the name, he felt it immediately from the tremor in her spine. His quest was at an end.

"How do you know my name?" Her whispered words tugged at Nico's heart. This was the first time he'd heard her speak, and just the sound of her quiet voice lanced through him.

"I came to Skithdron looking for you. Your sisters Alania and Belora, as well as your mother Adora, were recently found and reunited. They miss you, Riki."

Tears flooded her eyes and he pulled her gently closer, raising one manacled hand to soothe the hair back from her face as he crooned to her. His hands were bound together with strong chains, but he wasn't worried. The dragon inside him would break them easily enough.

"No one's called me that since I was little. No one knows my name."

"Except your family," Nico spoke softly, "and those of us who have been searching for you. I'm glad I found you."

Her beautiful eyes widened with hope, but then disillusionment shattered her expression. "But what good is it? We're both prisoners here."

Nico was glad to see some spirit still flared within her battered soul. She was of royal blood after all—as was he. Nico knew firsthand how hard it was to keep one of their kind down for long.

"Did Lucan say when he'd come back?"

"Not 'til morning. We probably have only a few more hours of peace at most."

"That'll be more than enough." Nico smiled at her confusion, a little hesitant about how to broach the next thing he must tell her. He decided to start off slowly. "Riki, your sister recently discovered she can, well...change. Do you know what I'm talking about?"

Riki shook her head. Nico didn't know if she was merely protecting herself or if she truly wasn't able to shift from human to dragon like her twin. But then, if she'd discovered how to shift, she would most likely have escaped long ago.

"Okay. Promise not to scream. I'm going to shift. It might frighten you, but I would never hurt you. Neither man nor dragon in my homeland would ever harm you, Riki. Do you believe me?"

"Dragon?" She paused. "My mother told us stories of a dragon she once knew."

"Ah yes, the infamous Lady Kelzy."

"Yes! Kelzy. That was her name." Riki smiled with obvious delight at the small memory of her youth returned to her.

"My name is Nico, and if you sit tight, I'll have us both out of these chains in a moment. Do you trust me enough to do that?"

Sitting up and hugging her knees, she nodded, though she was nibbling on her lips in worry. Unable to resist, Nico bent forward and kissed her forehead quickly. She jumped a little, but seemed encouraged by the small, comforting gesture. Moving back, Nico called forth the change and allowed the black mist to envelop his human form. He saw her eyes widen and then felt the manacles burst as his human hands changed to dragon scale, the iron of the chains unable to hold him. He heard Riki gasp, but overall, she was taking it well.

Sitting before her, he let her just look at him and tried to give her time to get used to his dragon form before he moved closer. He'd have to break her chains, leaving the cuffs intact for the moment. His talons were too sharp and too big to do such delicate work without hurting her, but he could definitely manage to snap the chains. The rest could be done once they were safely away.

"Nico?"

I'm here.

She clutched the sides of her head in confusion. "How'd you do that?"

You can do it too. Follow the path back to me in your mind, Riki.

She scrunched up her face so tight he had to try hard not to laugh.

Like this? Can you hear me?

I hear you, sweetheart. Well done. Now, don't be afraid. I'm going to move closer to break the chains, all right?

Riki held up the closest chain eagerly. Oh, she was game all right. Even as weak and tired as she was, she had a spirit that just wouldn't die. He admired that even as he guessed at the horrors she'd suffered at Lucan's hands. The mad king would pay, but first Nico had to get Riki to safety.

Working quickly, but as quietly at possible, Nico broke the chains as close to Riki's tender flesh as he could risk. Moving back, he shifted to human form once more.

We can still talk silently if you don't mind. It would be safer while we make our escape.

Is that what you meant when you said Lana had learned to shift? Can she become a dragon?

Nico headed toward the doorway as quietly as possible. They still had to get out of the palace and had little time left in the dark of night that would shield his black dragon form from eyes down below.

Yes. It was under dire circumstances and she's still a little awkward, but she can shift to dragon form. She's the first woman in centuries to be able to do so. I believe if anyone else can, it would be you, Riki. You're her twin after all. But don't worry if you can't. It is a rare, rare thing and we won't be disappointed in you if you can't shift. I promise you that.

I never knew such a thing was possible.

It's a secret, even in my land. The dragons know, but few humans are trusted with the knowledge.

Then I'm honored.

He liked the feel of her thoughts, so intimate in his mind. Rarely had he communicated with a human female in this fashion. There were so few women who could speak with dragons, they were each prized and protected by all knights and dragons in his land.

This woman would be doubly so. Not only could she hear and talk with dragons, she could probably heal them as well, or so their energy exchange led him to believe. Nico felt good, even after that dreadful torture session, and he knew he owed it all to Riki's incredible abilities and kind heart.

Did I thank you for healing me, sweetheart? He sought to distract her while he dealt with the guards. Two quick punches and the guards at the door were dispensed with. They would not wake for hours. *You've an amazing healing talent, milady.*

It's more like a curse. It's what's kept me a prisoner here.

She didn't even flinch as he led her past the unconscious guards. Nico admired her grit. She seemed to be ready for whatever might come. She looked fierce, but beneath the bravado he sensed a quaking fragility that touched his heart.

Nico took one of her hands in his as he led them up a narrow stair. She tugged hard on his hand, but he kept moving.

The castle gates are the other way. Her voice was a desperate whisper in his mind.

I know, but we've no need of doors. A tower ledge would be good or even an open window. We're flying out of here. They don't know I can shift and will never look for us in the sky.

But I can't fly!

He felt the panic in her mind and paused to bring her into his arms, calming her with his warmth.

You'll ride on my back, Riki. I promise I won't drop you or allow any harm to come to you. You'll see. You'll love flying once we're out of danger. I can almost guarantee it.

She calmed but seemed unconvinced. *How can you be so sure?*

He smiled down at her. *Because of your blood, my dear. Like me, you are part dragon.*

Are we related?

Only very distantly. You are of the House of Kent. My line descends from the House of Draneth.

Draneth the Wise?

Yes. Did your mother tell you tales of him when you were a little girl?

He kept her talking as they climbed higher and higher. He'd chosen this tower well. It was one of the highest in the castle and would provide a great launching point if they could reach the top without discovery.

No. I don't remember Mama talking about Draneth, but Lucan has all kinds of old manuscripts about him. He's obsessed with the man. He wants to be just like Draneth. That's why he made the deal with Salomar and the North Witch to make him...what he is now.

An abomination. Nico could not help the dark thunder in his thoughts but to her credit, Riki didn't flinch. He tried for a lighter tone as they kept moving upward. *Draneth had several children. The eldest continued his House and the younger ones founded great Houses of their own. Kent was the third son of Draneth if I remember correctly. You are descended from him.*

I never knew.

He reached the top stair where it led out to a landing. Pushing her to the wall below the floor line, he scoped out two sentries standing guard. He should have realized this highest tower would be a lookout position.

Stay here for a moment while I handle the guards.

She nodded while he slipped stealthily onto the open landing. The two men stood at opposite sides of the tower room, looking out huge, open windows with magnifying lenses trained on the grounds below. It was still too dark to see anything in the skies or anywhere that was not lit by the fires and lamps that accompanied human habitation, but Nico knew this position was a good vantage point during daytime to see for miles around.

He took down the first guard, dropping him as quietly as he could, but it wasn't quiet enough. The other sentry turned and reached for his horn to sound the alarm but he never got to it. Riki shot up the final few steps and tripped the soldier up so he fell part way down the stairwell, knocking himself out with a sharp crack to his skull on the stone treads.

"I thought I told you to stay put." Nico smiled as he faced her. There was a becoming bloom on her face and he once more admired her bravery.

"You looked like you could use a hand." She smiled and it transformed her face, stilling his heart for a timeless moment. Nico wanted desperately to see her smile again, and again and again. He could live for her smiles. He was disappointed when she turned away and surveyed the room and the open expanses of the giant spy windows.

"Dawn is coming soon. We don't have much time left." She faced him again, both serious and sad. "I want you to know, if we don't make it out of here... I wanted to thank you. I haven't been free in years and the last few months..." She sniffled delicately and it nearly broke his heart. "Well, it's been worse than before. Thank you for helping me escape. Lucan would never have let me go."

Crossing the room in two strides, Nico took her into his arms and kissed the crown of her head tenderly. He had to touch her, to hold her and give what reassurance he could.

"We'll make it, Riki. All you have to do is trust me. I promise. I won't let anything bad happen to you, now or ever again. You have my solemn vow."

Riki leaned back to look up at him and Nico kissed her again. As he tasted her lips with his own, there was an instant, blinding conflagration within his dragon soul. Inside, where his dragon slept while in human form, the beast stirred, trumpeting one word over and over in the dark recesses of his being.

Mine!

A slight noise from below finally penetrated and brought Nico back to the moment. He let her go, moving the fallen soldiers away from the opening so they would not be so readily visible from below. That might give them an extra few moments before the alarm was raised.

Holding her gaze, Nico moved away to let the change take him. The black mist rose and a moment later, he looked at her through the jeweled tourmaline eyes of his dragon form.

Climb on my back, sweetheart, he offered a bent foreleg for her to use as a step. She scrambled up and immediately flattened herself to his neck, wrapping her little arms around him and hugging him tight. He loved the feel of her, the way she clung to him and the heat of the secret place between her thighs over the ridge of his back, but he could not let it distract him. Not now.

They were still in danger. *Hold tight now. We'll fall for a bit at first until I can spread my wings fully, but don't worry. I've been flying for many years and haven't crashed yet.*

With a leap they were airborne and to her credit, Riki did not scream. Nico half-expected her to cry out in alarm, given the freefall required for him to launch from such a narrow opening. She clung tightly, but kept her mouth shut, which was all the better for their stealthy escape. There were other towers, he well knew, and other sentries who might notice the subtle beat of his wings. He skirted the towers as best he could but it was some moments before he breathed easier, flying out over open country.

Riki relaxed her death grip on his neck, obviously more comfortable with flying the farther away they got from the palace.

How are you doing, my lovely?

Right now I'm praying that this all isn't just a dream.

I can assure you, it's quite real. You're safe now. Or you will be as soon as we can get to the border.

Nico gained altitude as the night wore on. He knew the cold at this level was difficult for Riki, but better that than risk being seen. A dragon over the skies of Skithdron—particularly a royal black dragon—would bring out their enemies in force. He poured on the speed, hoping to go as far as possible before the sun rose too high in the sky. It was a long way to the border, but black dragons were the fastest of all dragons and Nico had trained himself to fly faster and longer than any of his brethren. Such skills were important in his line of work.

How are you doing, Riki?

I'm a little cold, but I'd rather be cold than dead.

Nico admired her spirit. He knew the heat produced by his body kept her warm for the most part, but she was poorly dressed for the altitude and much too thin as well. He would have to find her something better to wear during the daylight hours when flying would be too dangerous.

Snuggle in close to me, sweetheart. My body heat should help a bit.

Oh, it does. You're like a furnace, Nico. My own personal hot water bottle, on a giant scale.

Anytime, Riki. Again, he found himself chuckling. *I'll warm you anytime. All you have to do is ask.*

Chapter Three

As they flew through the night, Nico thought back to the mating flight he'd witnessed between his oldest brother, Roland, and his new queen. Lana was the first female black dragon in centuries and although she'd come to her wings later in life than most royal blacks, she trained hard and was flying beautifully by the time she and Roland tried to mate in dragon form. Lana didn't know it, but Roland had asked Nico to stand by in the shadows, watching in case Lana didn't come out of freefall in time.

Roland had convinced him the pleasure of being with his wife in any form was enough to overwhelm his senses and he was afraid her new flying reflexes weren't strong enough to save her should they wait too long to pull apart after climax. Roland wanted Nico there, as backup. So Nico watched as the first mated black dragon pair in centuries took their first mating flight, soaring to the stars together, joined in body and mind, then plummeting hard and fast to earth as they basked in the climax of their pleasure.

It had been beautiful. Wondrous. And it had sparked a tiny flame of jealousy in Nico's heart, though he refused to acknowledge it. Nico wanted that. Oh, he didn't think he'd ever find another female shapeshifter—Lana was the first in many generations—but he wanted that kind of love, that kind of bond with a woman. He and Roland were closer than most brothers, and he knew the extent of the bond between Roland's soul and his new wife's. Nico envied that bond. Not in a malicious way, but in a wistful, wishing sort of way.

Lana was a special woman, and a wonderful wife to his often lonely eldest brother. She was also proving to be a magnificent queen. Her heart was open and giving, her soul pure and deep. The people loved her as she was coming to love them and the dragons revered her like no human woman in centuries.

And Riki was her twin.

If any woman could survive the deprecations of being in Lucan's grasp, it was Riki. Though truthfully, Nico feared for her sanity. She seemed well enough, but he could only guess at the horrors she had seen and experienced as Lucan's captive. His heart nearly broke just thinking of it, and his was not a soft heart to bleed for every poor creature. Nico was a compassionate man, but not overly demonstrative. He kept his generosity well hidden, lest people try to curry favor with him simply because he had the ear and trust of the king.

Second in line to the throne of Draconia was a strange position. Nico had learned over the years to play his cards very close to his vest. He aided his brother where he could as provider of information, Spymaster and staunch ally. Roland had gained the throne so young after the brutal deaths of their parents. There was no question of Nico wanting such responsibility for himself. If, Mother forbid, something happened to Roland and Lana, Nico would step up to the challenge, but he didn't want it. He would much rather support his brother's reign.

Roland was a good and just king, surrounded by enemies in difficult times. Nico would put forth all his skills to see that

Roland not only succeeded in protecting the lands, people and dragons of Draconia, but kept his family and loved ones as safe as possible while doing it.

Bringing Riki home to her family was just one of the tasks Nico had undertaken. It might prove to be the noblest thing he'd ever done, but only time would tell. He already knew it was the one thing he'd done, so far in his life, of which he felt proudest.

Oh, he wasn't taking credit for stumbling over her, but rather he felt pride and wonder in *her*. Riki was down and beaten, but she clearly had never given up. He was glad he could fly, allowing them to escape easily from the nest of vipers Lucan called a palace. Nico was proud he could help her and amazed by the courage of the small woman clinging so desperately to life and probably to her sanity.

Nico flew on as long as he dared, but when dawn kissed the sky to the east, he knew it was time to find a safe place to land. His black wings would stand out too greatly against the day-lit sky. Plus, he was still somewhat drained from the torture session and beating the day before.

While Riki had managed to heal the worst of his hurts, he was not fully cured. Muscles protested each sweeping downbeat of his wings while recently healed slashes and burns pulled at his skin both on the surface and beneath. He'd had very little sleep and fatigue was creeping up on him no matter how hard he fought against it.

Riki was probably tired as well and would need a break. Nico had to find a safe place for them to pass the hours of daylight. Until they were able to leave Skithdron behind, they would travel by night, when his black dragon form would help them hide safely in the dark sky.

Nico kept a careful eye out for a likely place to rest and, before long, found a village. Not quite large enough to be considered a city, the place was still big enough that they could blend in with relative ease. There were also small fields with crops growing all around that would make good places to hide. There were only a few rocky outcroppings on the otherwise flat plain and the small tributary that wound through the area allowed some crops to be grown.

Nico picked a rock cluster, knowing most of the skiths that normally lived in such places had already been herded toward Draconia. He didn't see signs of the nasty creatures from the air, so he weighed his options as the sun peeped more fully over the horizon. He had to land. Quickly.

Setting down as gently as he could, Nico searched the rock formation fully while still in dragon form. As a dragon he could fight any remaining skiths and probably win, but if he were caught in human form, it would be difficult indeed. Finding no skiths, he scraped his belly along the ground to make it easier for Riki to climb down off his back.

Riki was bone weary as she stumbled down off the dragon's broad back. She'd been tired before, but not like this. This was a good kind of weariness that came after the greatest exhilaration Riki had ever known.

There was a stir of movement behind her and then two strong, human arms came around her, steadying her as she wobbled on her shaky legs. Nico. Her savior and her protector. A dragon in human form and a spinner of tales about her family. A bringer of hope.

But what manner of man was he, really? Riki had been too badly deceived by those she'd trusted before. So far, Nico had been all that was good and kind to her. Fierce when necessary, he was also gentle with her when she'd had so little gentleness in her life.

"Drink first," Nico said softly in her ear. She blinked open her sagging eyelids and saw his hand stretched in front of her, pointing toward a small stream. Suddenly she realized just how thirsty she was. "Then I can heat the little pool and you can have a bath, if you like." His hand moved slightly and Riki followed it with her gaze to a small area where the stream fed a shallow pond just to the right.

"That sounds like heaven."

Nico chuckled as he released her, slowly, as if to be certain her feet would support her. She stumbled toward the fresh, flowing water and sank to her knees on the soft bank. The water sparkled at her in the early morning light, beckoning her to drink her fill.

Riki didn't know how long she knelt at the stream's edge, repeatedly cupping water into her hand and bringing it to her mouth, but the cool freshness of the water roused her from her lethargy. She was aware of Nico drinking at her side. After a while, he moved off to rustle around behind her. Riki had no idea what he was doing, nor did she particularly care. No, at that moment all that mattered was the fresh, clean taste of the water against her tongue and the astounding feeling of freedom.

She hadn't been outside the palace walls in more than a year and hadn't seen the sun in months. Lucan kept her chained in his room and there hadn't even been a window for her to see the outside world.

"Now to get those manacles off you."

Riki looked up to find Nico standing at her side. She pushed back from the edge of the stream, but didn't—couldn't—rise. Her legs were numb. Nico crouched down next to her. He had two rocks in his hands. One was large and somewhat flat and the other was fist-sized with a sharp edge. He lay the rocks down next to her and took her hand, rubbing lightly at her sore wrists.

"I know these must hurt." His hushed words spoke straight to her heart. "But we'll get them off one way or another."

The manacle was welded shut around her wrist, with the remnants of chain trailing down her arm. Nico, in dragon form, had snapped the chains easily, but she realized why he'd left the delicate work 'til now once she'd seen his wickedly sharp dragon talons. Still, his strength had astonished her and continued to do so as he inserted the forefingers of both hands into the topmost link of the chain and pried it apart.

"That's amazing." Those were thick iron links. No man should be able to bend them as if they were malleable lead. She blinked up at him.

Nico chuckled. "One benefit of my heritage. Some of the dragon's strength remains even in human form. Now, let's see if this will work as well." He tossed the chain into the deep part of the stream and it was immediately swallowed up by the rocks below the surface. He then squeezed those same two fingers into the manacle, next to her sore skin. She couldn't help but wince when he rubbed a particularly sensitive welt, and he immediately stilled.

"I'm sorry, Riki." The look in his eyes spoke of anxiety over hurting her, however unintentionally.

"It's nothing. Please, keep trying. I'd suffer almost anything to have these things off my wrists, and you really didn't hurt me. I'm just a little sore."

He continued after a moment's pause, slower than before and twice as cautious. The idea that this big, strong man would temper his strength for her was humbling.

He pulled and pulled, but though the welded iron creaked a bit, it wouldn't give. Riki could see the bolt loosening, but it refused to break off, even under Nico's enormous strength. It was better than it had been, though.

"I think we need to try this another way." Nico removed his fingers easily now the manacle was looser, then took her hand to the ground, laying her wrist on the flat rock.

"What are you going to do?" She thought she had an idea, but she wanted to be sure.

"The rock here is some of the hardest in the world," he explained as he positioned her wrist just so. "I'm going to try to bust the head off that bolt and push it through, and then I should be able to bend the iron wide enough for you to wiggle your hand out. He lined up her hand, picking up the other rock in his fist. "Don't move now."

Riki held her breath as he swung the rock at her wrist, but his aim was true. The loud bang of rock against metal made her want to jump, but she knew how important it was to keep still. She'd learned every level of control over her body and emotions while being held by prisoner, so this was relatively easy to accomplish. Riki just kept the end goal in mind. Freedom for her aching, bloody, bruised and welt-ridden arms.

With a few more well-placed whacks, Nico's plan worked. The head came off the weakened bolt, and the shank fell through to the ground. Nico was able to wriggle his fingers inside and bend the iron wide enough for her hand to escape.

"One down." He smiled at her and she felt tears of joy slipping down her face as he rubbed her poor wrist. Bringing her wrist up to his lips, he placed a tender kiss on the bruised skin and then placed it gently in her lap, only to lift the other hand and repeat the process of removing the iron chain, then the manacle.

When both her hands were free of the heavy cuffs, Nico wet a square of linen he'd had in his pocket and washed her wrists with gentle pats and swipes, removing the grime and caked blood with the fresh, cold water. The care in his expression warmed her, but the little zing of his energy had her pulling her hands back.

"You can't!"

Nico sat back and looked at her. "I must, Riki. Please let me do what I can. I'm not much of a healer, but I can make you a little more comfortable at least."

She shook her head. "I know how tiring healing can be. You need your strength, Nico. There'll be time enough to heal after we're out of Skithdron once and for all."

But he scooped her hands up in his and pulled them into his lap, resting her palms on his knees. He held her wrists almost exactly where the manacles had been for so very long, but instead of hurting, Nico's hands were gentle and healing, as he poured little zaps of his own energy into her.

She was weak, but she felt her own power responding, rising, mingling with his and multiplying.

"Stop!"

"No, wait. It'll be okay, Riki. You'll see."

She tried to tug away, but it was too late. Their energies met and meshed, concentrating healing energy on her poor, abused wrists, but oddly, it wasn't draining. Not much anyway. And her own energy seemed to be working on her injuries, which it never had before.

"What's happening?"

Nico pulled back, letting her wrists go with a broad smile. They were healed. Completely healed for the first time in months.

"I thought this might work." He blinked with fatigue, but she couldn't see the bone-weary tiredness that always came after she performed a healing of this magnitude.

"What did you do?"

"It's something that happened to me only once before. Riki, I've never been a strong healer, but when your mother was hurt, I tried to help and her energy rose to direct me, just as yours did a moment ago. Kelzy said it's our blood recognizing each other. I would never have managed this level of healing on my own, but with your energy to guide me, it was possible."

"I've never been able to heal myself before."

Nico shook his head with a sigh. "Most healers can't. You probably still won't be able to do so, but if we mesh our energies, some of your skill guides and amplifies my own power. At least, that's my guess as to what happened."

"You did this with my mother, you said?"

Nico stood and tossed the rock away. "I did. She'd been clawed by a dragon, accidentally of course. Kelzy felt terrible about it, but it was the only way to save your mother's life. At the time she was clinging to the top of a tree with a horde of skiths circling below. Kelzy had to grab for her, but it's hard to be accurate with such sharp talons. She saved Adora, but wounded her in the process."

Riki still couldn't believe he was talking about her mother. Her mother! Alive and living in Draconia, reunited with the dragon from her childhood who'd been like a mother to her. It was a dream come true, and Riki was almost afraid to believe she might be reunited with her mother and sisters—if they made it out of Skithdron alive.

Riki marveled at her healed wrists as she drank a bit more water from the flowing stream. Distracted by a whooshing sound, Riki turned toward the small pool off to her right. Nico smiled over at her, his face so handsome, it made her stomach clench.

"Your bath is ready, milady."

Riki stared mutely, unable to move, until Nico came to her and lifted her by the shoulders.

"Are you all right?"

Riki nodded, unable to form the words for the feelings inside her. Confusion, fear that this moment of freedom wouldn't last, thankfulness to this wonderful, perplexing man, and more churned within her.

Nico put his arm around her shoulders and guided her to the small pool. Incredibly, she could see little tendrils of steam wafting off its surface.

"It's warm now and will stay that way for a while. I suggest you hop in if you want to bathe. I'll turn my back if you like, but I won't leave you. Not even for a moment." He surprised her by placing a chaste kiss on her temple. "I won't let anything harm you ever again, Arikia."

The whispered words and the way he said her name caused a tremor to course through her. He let go and turned away, leaving Riki to decide her next move. The steamy water called to her and she realized she hadn't bathed properly in far too long. Not even bothering to remove her thin dress, she stepped into the small pool and immersed herself in the shallow water.

It was heaven. Riki just lay there for a few moments allowing the warm water to surround her and warm her. Flying atop a dragon in the dead of night had left her chilled through and through, but she'd never complain. The cold flight meant freedom and that was too precious to complain about.

After a few minutes of warm bliss, Riki looked around to find a plant she was familiar with from her youth growing along the pond's edge. Scrubweed, it was called. It didn't lather like soap, but the sinuous blades, when wound together, made an excellent sort of sponge and emitted a slippery substance that cleaned almost as well as soap.

Looking to make sure Nico's back was turned, Riki pulled the wet dress over her head, letting it soak in the water for a bit. First she wanted to get clean herself. Then she'd wash the dress. Riki grabbed handfuls of the scrubweed blades and wound them into hand-sized pads. Sweeping the slightly abrasive plant fibers over her skin had never felt so good. The warm water, the soothing green scent of the scrubweed and the heady feeling of freedom combined into a sparkling moment of happiness.

Riki giggled as she washed herself, uncontrollably happy and giddy as a child.

"Sounds like you're having fun." Nico's voice floated to her as he sat on a rock, facing away from her. He was being quite the gentleman and she was touched by his chivalry.

"I haven't taken a bath in so long. And not in warm water since I was a child."

"Sometimes it's handy to be a dragon." His tone teased.

"I bet." Riki started to work on her dress, cleaning it as best she could. It would be soaking wet when she put it back on, but it couldn't be helped. Unless...

"Nico, can you produce enough heat to dry my dress?" Her words were hesitant and shy, but also curious.

"Throw it over here and I'll see what I can do." His wry chuckle sounded as she rolled the thin dress into a ball and took aim.

Unfortunately, she smacked him right in the head with the wad of sopping fabric, but he only laughed as he unwound the mess from his neck and laid it out over the rock he'd been sitting on. He touched the rock with both hands, and within moments, steam started to rise from the wet material.

"That's amazing."

Nico looked over at her and winked. Riki was glad she was still immersed in the water, but the look in his eyes was teasing, not predatory. Still, she was relieved when he turned back around so he couldn't see her. After a few more moments, he lifted the dress by the shoulders and it looked mostly dry.

"I think that's about as good as I can get it." He tilted his head as if considering the simple dress, then squared his shoulders. "I'm turning around now."

Riki gasped as he turned, his gaze traveling over what he could see of her naked body beneath the water. She crossed her arms over her breasts though Nico didn't seem threatening. No, his hot gaze was more admiring than dangerous. Still, there was fire in his eyes, heat in the way he stalked closer to her, holding her dress out before him.

"It will do you no good to have a dry dress if you put it on over wet skin." His voice was a sultry rumble. "Come out of there, sweetheart, and let me dry you."

Gathering her courage, Riki tried to decide what to do. This man was tempting in the extreme. He'd saved her, he'd taken care of her to this point, but could she trust him not to try to take more from her than she was willing to give? If she lost her virginity, she lost everything—her power, her safety, and most probably her life if Lucan ever found her. But this man was temptation itself.

Handsome, thoughtful, kind and incredibly strong, he was appealing on every level. He'd suffered Lucan's torture with a dignity she'd never seen before and a courage that put her to shame. He was such a noble, brave being, and such a magical one. She had to keep reminding herself Nico was half dragon. It was incredible. Even after riding on his strong back for hours in the inky night sky, she could hardly believe it was all real.

“Come on, sweetheart. You know I’d never harm you. It would kill me to see you hurt in any way.” He shook the dress invitingly, his dark, hazel eyes watching her reactions carefully.

Riki couldn’t deny him. Tucking away her self-doubts and her fear, she rose hesitantly from the cooling water to stand before the man who had quite literally saved her life. Without him, she would still be back in Lucan’s palace. She owed him so much, yet he treated her as if she were precious. The thought humbled her. Nico was proving himself to be a man of honor in every way. She just hoped she could resist his charm enough to retain her virginity and with it, her power. Without that, she was too vulnerable. It was the only thing of value she had and it would be suicide to allow it to be lost.

Yet something inside her yearned for this man. She wanted to know him—to know what his lovemaking would feel like. He stirred things in her she’d thought long dead and curiosities better left alone.

Chapter Four

Riki stepped from the pond to stand before him and Nico's mouth went dry. She was so beautiful, even skinny and hurt as she was. Her poor, little, battered body touched something deep inside him. Nico knew what she would look like when her wounds were healed and she was healthy once more. He had, after all, seen her twin sister Lana naked in the bath with his older brother, Roland.

While he'd admired Lana's smooth curves and womanly form, she didn't stir him like this. No, there was something special about Riki. She affected him like no woman ever before, on so many different levels. She was malnourished and bruised now, but he saw the beauty of her soul, the purity of her spirit shining through those lovely green eyes. He knew, given half a chance and some time to heal, Riki could easily make him her willing slave.

Not allowing himself a moment's more temptation, Nico handed her the dress and shifted to dragon form. If he stayed in his human form, he'd drag her into his arms. He simply didn't trust himself not to ravish her, and he could see from the hesitant curiosity in her eyes that she would welcome his advances—or at least he could make her welcome them with a little coaxing. It was one of the things Nico did best, coaxing people to do his bidding, but he refused to take Riki that way.

No, if she came to his bed, she would come of her own volition, of her own free will. That was the only way he could be sure of her, certain she would be completely his.

And suddenly, that was the most important thing in his world.

Sucking in a deep breath, Nico puffed warm air over Riki's wet skin, admiring the way her little nipples stood at attention. She was so beautiful. After a moment of shyness, Riki held the dress out to her side so his warm dragon breath could float over her whole body. She turned around so he could dry her back and he had to appreciate the sight of her pert bottom.

There were lash marks, too, crisscrossing her back, that fired his anger. Lucan would pay for what he'd done to this woman. *His* woman.

"Why are you growling? Is something wrong?" Riki craned her neck around to look at him and Nico knew he had to get his rage under control.

It's nothing, he answered in her mind, glad when she pulled the thin dress over her head. He shifted quickly to human form, pulling her back into his arms, hugging her tight. "No one will ever beat you again, Arikia."

The words shivered through him, a vow he would not break. His arms trembled as he held her against his chest, his arms as gentle as he could make them around her waist and shoulders.

"It's all right, Nico."

Her voice soothed the raging anger in his soul. Nico kissed her damp hair with tender desperation. What he was feeling inside was bigger than anything he'd ever felt before. His dragon soul was roaring for its mate while his human heart trembled in awe at the thought this delicate creature might actually be the woman he'd been searching for all his life.

"I'm not much of a healer, Riki, but when we're out of danger, I'll do my best to see those marks are removed and every last scar healed. I only wish I could make it so you'd never suffered at all."

She turned in his arms, surprising him and testing his control. It was all he could do not to kiss her and take her to the ground beneath him. He wanted her desperately.

But her safety and comfort had to come first. This was no time for Nico to let his base desires overrule his common sense. He had to remain alert for any danger. This was Skithdron after all. Danger came in many forms in this land.

Lucan was also sure to be looking for them. The crazy king would not suffer their escape happily. No, he would send his guards after them. He would spread word throughout the land, searching for them.

Nico had to be on guard. Certainly, in his role as Spymaster of Draconia, he'd been in dire straits before, but this time was different. This time, it wasn't just his own skin at stake, and he refused to take any chances with Riki's precious life. She pressed close to his chest, gazing up at him as if she could see right into his soul.

"Thank you, Nico, but you've got to save your strength. We need to get out of Skithdron as quickly as possible."

Her words brought him back to his senses. "You'll get no argument from me on that score, milady. But first, we have to rest. And then we need to secure some food and perhaps some warmer clothing for you."

"But where?"

"We're near a large town." He nodded toward his left as he let her pull away from him, little by little. It was hard to let her go, but he knew he had to do so. "After we rest, just before sundown, we'll go into the village and get what we need."

"But we don't have any money."

Nico grinned as she moved away and sat on the rock he'd used before. "I could steal what we need, but as it happens," he lifted his left foot and opened a secret compartment in the sole of his boot, "I do have some coin left."

Riki leaned over to look at the footwear more closely. "That's ingenious!"

Nico bowed slightly. "Thank you. I thought so too. Lucan's men took my purse and all other items of value, but I always try to have a stash available for emergencies such as this."

"You do this kind of thing often, then?" Her teasing smile enchanted him.

Nico shrugged. "Often enough. It's one of the hazards of being a spy."

He watched her reaction closely. He'd never told a woman the truth of his profession before, but this woman was different. Her reaction mattered to him. It nearly sickened him to think she might be horrified by the idea, but he needn't have worried. Her beautiful eyes lit with sparks of interest and a kind of daring intrigue mirroring the way he felt about the work he performed in service to his land and people.

"I knew there was something special about you."

Her casual acceptance seeped into his heart and warmed his soul. "You're the special one, milady. I'm but a humble soldier in service to my king."

"You work for the king of Draconia?"

Nico nodded as he pocketed just a few of the spare coins in his shoe, leaving the rest hidden. "He's my brother."

"Your brother? So does that make you a prince?" She paused. "Good gods! You're *Prince* Nicolas."

He bowed his head, laughing at her stunned reaction. "The very same."

"Lucan is a fool. He had no idea who you were."

"All the better for me. If he'd known—"

"If he'd known," she cut him off, her voice somber, "you'd already be dead. He hates the royal family of Draconia. He's insanely jealous of you all and wants every last one of you dead. He rants about it, even when he's alone. It's an obsession of his."

"I feared as much. We've learned only recently about his machinations even before he was crowned, and all evidence points to the fact that he's been working for years to destroy every royal line in Draconia. Including yours."

"Me?" She laughed nervously. "I'm not royal."

"I beg to differ. Rightfully, you are Princess Arikia of the House of Kent."

"You must be joking!"

He smiled at her, enjoying her soft manner, even when outraged. "Afraid not. Your mother was the only survivor when her entire family was murdered. I believe that was done at Lucan's command, though I may never be able to prove it. As far as we've been able to determine, a maidservant took your mother, who was just a baby at the time, and ran off the very night of the massacre. She raised your mother, renaming her and keeping her as her own, so she never knew of her birthright, but yet she had an affinity for dragons that led her—even as a toddler—to the dragoness, Kelzy."

"So you're saying my mother is like you? Half-dragon?"

"As you are. All the members of the various royal lines carry the dragon as part of their soul. All the descendants of Draneth are half dragon, and therefore royal. Your line descends from Kent, third son of Draneth, so like it or not, you're a princess of Draconia." She didn't look convinced.

"I suppose we're cousins, then?" She seemed to be thinking out loud.

Nico moved close to her, sweeping one arm around her waist and pulling her lithe form up against his chest. He liked the little gasp she emitted at his sudden move. He liked even more that she didn't make the slightest attempt to pull away.

"Only if we're kissing cousins, my lovely Arikia." He placed a sweet kiss on her lips, hesitating only a moment before taking it deeper, claiming her mouth with his own.

She tasted of violets and springtime...and the need for possession. He would give anything to make her his own, for all time, but he couldn't rush her. Nico knew he had to do this right. This was, perhaps, the most important seduction of his life and he would be damned sure to give her the time she needed to come to him of her own volition. Remembering his goal, he drew back, though it was one of the hardest things he'd ever done.

"You're a wonder to me, Arikia. So strong, so feminine, so beautiful in spirit and heart."

The blush staining her cheeks touched him. This little woman wasn't used to compliments of any kind, he realized. He would have to remedy that and make her understand her beauty—both inner and outer—by reminding her every day for the rest of their lives. It was a duty he would not only enjoy, but relish.

Stepping back, he released her slowly.

"Any other questions?"

She seemed to consider for a moment.

"Where do your clothes go when you shift?"

Nico couldn't help it. He burst out laughing. Of all the questions he'd expected, that one took him by surprise.

"I don't know exactly where they go, but back when I was first learning how to shift, they didn't always come back." He chuckled as her eyes widened and dropped down his body, giving him the once over. "It's part of the magic Draneth the Wise brokered between dragon and humankind."

"He was a wizard, wasn't he?"

Nico nodded. "One of the last in this realm. He gave up his command of the greater magics to become human—and dragon—though some of his lesser magics have passed down the royal lines through his children and their descendants for hundreds of years. I can't conjure items from thin air, but if I had something on my person at the time I shifted—like those coins in my shoe—I can summon them back when I shift back." Nico noted the position of the sun in the sky. "Now we should rest for a few hours." Brushing a small area in the crevice between two natural walls of stone that formed a slight angle and would protect them somewhat, Nico motioned for her to lie down on the sandy ground.

Riki did so without complaint and it again struck home to Nico how this poor little waif had not had much comfort in her young life. She seemed unaware of the hardness of the ground against her body, but settled in as if she were used to sleeping on the floor. And indeed, Nico realized sadly, she probably was.

After a last check, Nico lay down next to her. She trembled a bit, and he could almost taste her fear, but he would protect her from all danger. Even from himself.

"Rest easy, little one." He crooned to her, pulling her small body back against his with one strong arm around her waist. "I won't hurt you. I'm just going to hold you and keep you safe."

He also hoped for some of that remarkable healing energy exchanging between them as they slept and making them both stronger. It wasn't guaranteed, he knew, but they had to be touching in order for it to have a chance at working.

But touching is all he would do.

Even if it killed him.

No matter how badly he wanted—no, *needed*—to roll her beneath him and slide home into her warm depths. He couldn't. He wouldn't. No, she had to come to him. That's the only way he could bind her to him for the rest of their lives and beyond. By her own free will.

That thought firmly in mind, Nicolas spooned her into his body, stroking her hair and soothing her as best he could. Trust had to be earned, he well knew, and this was the first step. He would hold her as they slept and she would learn she could trust him with her safety, her body, and yes, her virginity.

"Nico—"

He refused to hear her objections. This was too important.

"Hush, sweetheart. Trust me. All I want to do is hold you. That's all. This is how you'll learn to trust me. I promise you."

"I'm not used to this."

"Yet you slept nestled against me in Lucan's chamber and came to no harm. Trust me in this, sweetheart. I will never, ever harm you. It would kill me to hurt you."

"You don't even know me," she objected. "Sometimes I feel like I don't even know myself." That last was a whispered confession as he felt her tremble against him.

Nico held her tighter, soothing her as best he could while she shook with emotion. He thought she might even be crying, and he knew that was probably a good thing. After all she'd been through, Riki needed to let a little of the hurt out.

"It's all right, baby. I've got you. And I know all I need to know about you." He kissed the crown of her head. "I know you are a good, caring, giving person. You healed me when you didn't really need to do more than keep me alive for Lucan's next round. You have the courage of a knight and the heart of a dragon. You, who have never flown before, trusted me enough to take a leap of faith of the highest turret in Skithdron into the black of night and never once complained."

She chuckled then and it was a watery sound. She *was* crying, and it nearly broke his heart.

"That wasn't courage. That was fear of being recaptured." She grew stiff once more as she whispered, "I'd rather have died."

"No, sweetheart. Never think that. Where there's life, there's hope. And wherever you are, there I'll be, ready to help you in whatever way I can. I promise you that. Now and forever."

"You're a kind man, Nico."

"Oh, please don't let that get around. It would ruin my reputation as a scoundrel."

She chuckled again and this time the sound was more lighthearted and less sad.

"A kind scoundrel, then. Is that better?"

"Just a bit," he agreed, kissing her hair and settling her into his warmth. Already he could feel their energies reaching for one another. They both needed this healing sleep more than anything right now and he was gratified to feel her begin to relax, her body finding its way into restful oblivion.

Waking hours later, Nico quickly scanned the area. Riki slept on, in the same position she'd been in when she'd fallen asleep. She was so peaceful in his arms, he hated to move, but he had work to do.

Nico knew it had been a risk for them both to sleep, but it was a necessary risk. The fatigue of the beating, then escape, coupled with the healing he'd done on her wrists had been more than even he could bear, and he had to be strong to get them both the rest of the way to safety, across the border to Draconia.

Judging by the sun's position, it was mid-afternoon. Nearly perfect timing for what he had planned. Rising with more than a little regret, Nico stalked a short distance away where his dragon senses told him a rabbit was nibbling on succulent grasses near the bank of the stream. It wasn't much, but Riki had been starved almost beyond bearing. When she woke from her sleep, he wanted to have food for her and this rabbit would do nicely as a start. The rest he would pick up in the town, if the Mother of All continued to bless their path.

Giving up a silent prayer to Her for providing the rabbit and watching over their safety, Nico pounced. Just a few minutes later, with the judicious application of sharp talons and a few puffs of dragon flame, the meat was cooked and ready.

The scent of roasting meat woke Riki from a blessedly dreamless sleep. She hadn't felt so good upon rising in years. Blinking open her sleepy eyes, Riki saw the provider of her well-being.

Nico.

He was even more handsome in the fading light of the sun than he had been in the dawn, and the smile he sent her way simply stole her breath.

"Breakfast is served, milady." He bowed with a comical flourish, bringing over the sizzling meat, still skewered from cooking, though she didn't see a fire.

"How did you cook that?"

"Riki," he clicked his tongue at her with a teasing smile, "I'm a *dragon.*"

She had to laugh at that. It had been so long since she'd had anything to laugh about. It felt good to be carefree—or almost so—for the first time in years. And it was all thanks to this incredible man.

Riki reached out and took the skewer of meat from him.

"Thank you, Prince Nicolas."

"Ah, it's just Nico to you, my dear. Besides, we're still in hostile territory. Nick the Spy is who I am when outside the borders of my homeland."

Riki nodded gravely, realizing all too well how important it was that his true identity remain a secret. If Lucan ever got wind of exactly who and what Nico was, he would move heaven and earth to kill him. Not that Lucan wasn't probably already moving heaven and earth to get her back. She knew how important she was to his continued existence.

Without a healer at his beck and call, the skith blood and venom inside Lucan would begin to kill him, slowly, painfully, and terribly. She felt a slight pang for what he would suffer, but she relished her freedom. Going back was not an option. She'd die rather than be recaptured.

"Eat, sweetheart. It's nearly time for us to make our move on the town."

Riki bit into the perfectly cooked rabbit, enjoying her first taste of meat in months. Lucan hadn't allowed her to eat well, throwing her scraps from his table only rarely. Most often, she was fed by a slave who brought her gruel once a day from the palace kitchens. It was nearly unpalatable stuff, but she knew Lucan kept her weak on purpose so she'd be more biddable.

She wolfed down the portion, savoring each bite though she couldn't help but eat fast. She was starving. Only now, with food in front of her, did she allow herself to feel the true extent of her hunger.

"Aren't you going to have any?"

Nico shook his head, passing her the rest of the rabbit. "I'll get something in town."

He crouched down opposite her, smiling so kindly, it made her knees weak.

"Please, I feel like a glutton. Won't you have some?"

She held the skewer out to him and he seemed to consider it for a short moment before leaning even closer. He snapped at it with his teeth, holding her gaze as he tugged a piece from the skewer in her hand. For some reason, his actions made her breathless, her gaze imprisoned by his as he chewed, swallowed, then licked his lips with a slow, sensuous glide of his tongue.

"Delicious."

Somehow she got the impression he was talking about more than just the meat. His hand lifted, covering hers gently and guiding the skewer back towards her mouth as he watched her.

"Eat up, sweetheart. We need to get moving soon."

Nico jerked back suddenly, his head cocked toward the road a short distance to their left, behind the towering rocks. Nobody could see them from the road, nor could Nico and Riki see much unless they climbed a bit higher on the rocks, but they could hear pretty well. Sound carried over the barren landscape of this part of Skithdron.

Fear shivered through Riki as she became aware of frightening noises. The jingle of tack meant horses, and the galloping sound of their hooves indicated they were traveling fast. Metal clanks made her think of the swords, shields and light armor favored by some of Lucan's guards.

Riki said not a word as Nico straightened. He climbed just high enough to see over the rocks to the road while Riki sat still as stone and worried. Her ragged fingernails bit into her palms as she clenched her fists, every muscle in her body screaming silently in terror they would be discovered.

Nico dropped down on nearly silent feet. His face was grim, but his stance seemed mostly relaxed.

"We're safe for now, but those were palace guards, which can't be good for us. They're heading for the town. That means you can't be seen there, Riki, but we badly need supplies."

"Then what can we do?"

"I'll go in alone. There's less chance they'll recognize me. I have ways to blend in and I can fight them off better than you if they do catch me. But that means we'll have to stash you someplace safe first."

"You make it sound so easy."

"It's anything but, sweetheart. But we'll make this work. Never fear."

Riki caught movement out of the corner of her eye. It was slithering and it was huge.

"Nico!"

Her terrified whisper had him turning even before the last syllable left her lips. He faced the giant skith sliding toward them from across the small pond and morphed quickly and cleanly into his dragon form. Nico put himself between Riki and the deadly creature.

Nico breathed in a lungful of air and let loose with a torrent of flame that warmed her even from ten feet away. He advanced on the skith, giving no quarter as the giant creature tried to evade and spit its deadly venom at him. But it had little immediate effect on dragon scale. Riki knew Nico could stand against a single skith for some time before the venom would eat through even his tough dragon hide. One on one, dragons were usually stronger than skiths, or so the bards said.

Still, he had to be in some pain from the acid on his scales. The skith was wily, but Nico advanced, not allowing it to retreat or get in more shots than he could handle. With a final blast of powerful flame, he roasted the creature until it stopped moving, dead.

Nico, in dragon form, used his talons to stab through the carcass to be certain of its demise. Skiths were dangerous and hard to kill, even for a dragon. When he appeared satisfied the creature was dead, Nico immediately rolled his sleek black dragon body into the nearby stream, washing off the venom as best he could.

"Are you all right?"

I'm fine, sweet. The venom just stings a little. The water will wash it away and I'll be good as new in a few minutes.

Riki found her feet and scurried over to help him, splashing water from upstream, where it was clear, onto his glistening scales as he wallowed in the shallow stream. She saw rough spots where the venom had begun eating away at his remarkably tough but flexible hide and concentrated her work on those spots first. After a few minutes, Nico stood from the stream, shaking off the last of the water.

"How do you feel?"

Nico transformed before answering. "Good as new."

And he did indeed look unharmed as he stood before her, dressed once again in his leather breeches and shirt.

"That was amazing."

Weak now with relief, Riki began to sag, but Nico caught her in his strong arms and hugged her close for a moment.

"I'm sorry to have scared you, baby." His words whispered into the hair by her ear. "I'm so sorry to have put you in danger."

She pulled back to look into his pained eyes. "That wasn't your fault, Nico. We're in Skithdron. Skiths are a common enough hazard in this cursed land. You can't be blamed for that. But I can thank you for saving my life, yet again."

She reached up, daringly, and kissed his lips. She so wanted his kiss after what they'd just been through. He was such a good, brave and courageous man, yet so gentle with her. If she wasn't much mistaken, she was half in love with him already.

Oh, this man was dangerous indeed.

Riki pulled away before either of them could deepen the kiss, knowing it was for the best. She couldn't give up her virginity for anything. Not yet. Not until she was safely away from Skithdron and out of Lucan's reach.

Nico watched her as if he would say something, but shrugged and let her go. He made a show of surveying their surroundings and gauging the time from the sun before turning back to her.

"We'd best be going. Anyone who sees this will know a dragon was responsible. And the smell will carry. Luckily the wind is blowing away from the town, or we'd be done for."

She hadn't thought of that, but realized he was right. "All right then, let's go. The sooner we get this over with, the sooner we can get out of Skithdron."

"Truer words have never been spoken, sweetheart." Nico winked at her as they walked into the sparse trees that lined the road. "We'll walk parallel to the road, but not on it. We don't want to be seen until after I've found a place to stash you, then I'll double back and enter from the road so any townsfolk who see me won't be suspicious."

"Good plan."

"Hey, this is what I do, Arikia. It's my job."

"And I see you're very good at it." She smiled at him, truly glad for his presence on this journey. Without him she wouldn't have made it three feet outside Lucan's door. For that matter, she would never have escaped at all. She'd still be chained to Lucan's bed, serving his perverse pleasure.

They arrived near the outskirts of the sizeable town before long, just as the sun made its journey toward the distant horizon. The sparse trees gave way to cultivated fields closer to town. Rows of tall corn stood against the pink and orange sky. Rays of the setting sun silhouetted Nico's strong features against the bright orange and red horizon.

He was so handsome, she had to catch her breath every time she took a moment to think about how beautiful he was—both inside and out. So far he had been all that was kindness to her and his valor was unquestioned. Nico had faced down Lucan's torture, his guards, and just now a deadly skith, without any weapon except his amazing ability to transform into a dragon.

Riki trusted him with her life and knew, deep down, she would give him her heart as well, with little protest, if he but asked. Still, she had to guard against letting him know how easily he could make her fall in love with him. Nico was a rogue. Worse than that, he was a prince of royal blood and no matter that he said she was some long-lost noble of Draconia, Riki would always be nothing more than a runaway slave. She could never have Nico in her life. Nor would he, in all probability, want her for more than a few precious days.

Better they remain friends and comrades. Better for her physical safety and the safety of her fragile, untried heart.

"This ought to do," Nico mused as he looked at their surroundings. "It'll be dark soon and these fields are probably your best bet for concealment, but I want you to have an escape route should you need it. If a skith comes along—"

"I'll run like hell."

Nico chuckled softly. "I like your attitude, sweetheart. That's good. But skiths are pretty fast. Even your lovely feet won't carry you fast enough. But what you can do is climb."

"Climb what?"

"See that tree over there?"

They were on the edge of the cornfield now, closest to the town. In fact, the field backed up to the walls of the town, which were formed by the backs of barns, houses and sheds with planking between to keep the skiths out. The tree Nico pointed out was just on this side of the wall, right next to a barn with a slightly sloping roof.

"I see it, but I should warn you, I haven't climbed a tree since I was eight years old."

"If a skith is chasing you, you'll climb all right. Fear for one's life is a wonderful motivator."

That sobered her. She had lived the last years in nearly constant fear for her life. And Nico was right—fear was a good motivator. He must've seen her expression in the dimming twilight because he scooped her into his arms and hugged her for a quick moment.

"I'm sorry, sweetheart." He kissed the crown of her head softly, almost apologetically, and his tenderness made her want to cry. But this was no time for hysterics. They had to get in and out of here as quickly as possible.

"It's all right, Nico. Really. So, you want me to climb that tree?"

He let her go with a final kiss to her hair. "Yes, but only if you need to. Climb the tree, then scoot back onto the roof as close to the peak as possible. No skith will be able to get you there, and you should be out of spitting range."

"Then why don't I just go up there now, while you go into town?"

"Because you might be seen. Even at night, people travel the road and farmers keep odd hours to bring in their herds. Don't go up there unless you need to, all right?"

She nodded as understanding sank in. The tree was a good ten yards from the edge of the field. "So you want me to stay here in the corn until I sense danger, then sprint for the tree and then the roof. Right?"

He beamed down at her, brimming with approval. "You're a quick one."

"Not really." Riki felt her cheeks flush and ducked her head as Nico cupped her cheek.

"You're a beautiful, intelligent woman, Arikia." He spoke so earnestly, she had to look up into his sparkling eyes. "Don't ever doubt that."

He kissed her sweetly then, not taking the kiss deeper, just a tender salute to her lips that meant so much to her bruised, battered heart. Releasing her too soon, Nico stepped back and watched her, his gaze nearly burning her with its intensity.

"I have to go, but I'll be back within an hour. I promise."

Fear set in as she watched him backing away. "Hurry back, Nico."

His expression softened for a moment. "I will. Stay safe and be alert. I'll be back before you know it."

And with that, he melted away into the darkening stalks of corn.

Chapter Five

Leaving Riki in that cornfield was one of the hardest things Nico had ever done, but he could see no other way. Backtracking quickly, he headed for the road, glad full dark was almost upon him. Nothing could delay him with Riki waiting in the cold, dangerous gloom of a Skithdronian eve. He had to move fast.

Nico offered up a silent prayer to the Mother of All for Riki's safety and his own as he took the path to town, out on the road in the open for the first time in days. Nico was taking a very great risk, going into a town where he knew Lucan's soldiers had already, no doubt, spread word of their escape. Holding his breath, Nico was pleasantly surprised when he made it past the sleeping gatekeeper with little fuss. People were walking back and forth through the large gate without anyone questioning who they were or what they were doing in the fortified town.

Gates and walls around towns were standard in Skithdron to keep out the skiths. Unchecked, a skith could ravage a town like this in short order, but the resourceful people of this land had learned to build their homes in clusters, leaving strong, blank walls around the place, composed of the backs of buildings with huge log fences in the spaces between. They were uncommonly good at keeping skiths out and people in, hence the need for a gate. The gatekeeper was supposed to watch for skiths and drop the heavy door at first sight, sealing the town and raising the alarm. The side effect, of course, was that a nosey gatekeeper could also regulate who went in and out of the town.

This gatekeeper, however, seemed more interested in watching the insides of his own eyelids than the road or environs. He was snoring softly as Nico passed, sprawled in his chair next to the rope and pulley system that would lower the gate swiftly if danger threatened.

Moving unobtrusively, Nico found a likely tavern in short order. The innkeeper was a rotund man with red cheeks and an overall jolly look to him. He eyed Nico suspiciously at first, but brightened when he saw the silver coin Nico offered for fast, efficient, *discreet* service.

Nico ordered a large basket of food. He surveyed the room, spying a worn, black, woolen cloak hanging in a corner behind the counter.

"That looks to be a warm cloak." Nico kept his voice low so as to not be overheard. "I lost mine on the road and was hoping to find a replacement. Is it for sale?"

The man's gaze shot to the bar across the room and Nico's followed. Two young men manned the long bar, both sharing the innkeeper's strong features. Undoubtedly, they were his sons and the cloak probably belonged to one of them.

"Losing one's cloak is a sorry thing," the man said, pursing his lips for dramatic effect as he frowned. Nico palmed another coin, allowing the innkeeper to glimpse the gleaming gold in his hand. "But I believe we could come to an arrangement, seeing as how the days are growing colder."

"Do you have any sturdy rope? I could use some of that as well."

The man's eyes narrowed. "I have some in back."

The man was not only shrewd, but a bit opportunistic. Nico didn't want to risk asking for clothes for Riki. He'd done well enough for now. He watched the room as the innkeeper bustled around behind him, packing the basket with food and the other items.

The innkeeper seemed more than happy to earn such a large sum for comparatively little and hustled everything together in record time while Nico tucked into a quick, hot bowl of stew. He was about halfway through with the meal when two of Lucan's castle guards came stalking through the door, taking seats at a table just a few feet from Nico.

He took the opportunity to listen in on their conversation, doing his best to appear calm and nonchalant. When the door had first opened, Nico thought he was done for, but the guards seemed more interested in eating and drinking than rousting the patrons of the tavern. Thank the Mother.

Nico breathed a sigh of relief when the guards set into their hearty meals and the landlord returned with the cloak and basket. Making a strategic retreat, Nico calmly left the tavern, one gold coin lighter, but richer in both provisions and information. He'd heard quite a bit of the guards' grousing and knew with certainty now the alarm had been sent up from here to the border.

Lucan's fast action spelled trouble for their ability to cross the border, but Nico decided to take things one step at a time. First he had to supply them for the journey as best he could, then he would see about getting them out of Skithdron.

Spying a likely clothesline, Nico also took the opportunity on his way out of town to pilfer a bit of clothing for Riki. She had to have been frozen after the long, cold ride the night before. Leaving a silver coin in payment, Nico felt no guilt for taking the unknown peasant woman's dress.

He circled back cautiously through the cornfield, knowing darkness brought out predators in Skithdron the likes of which they didn't see in his native land. Still, Nico was traveled enough to know how to avoid the worst of them, and he used all his skills now as he made his way quickly back to Riki.

Nico arrived back at the spot where he'd left Riki, but she was nowhere to be found. Panic threatened until a rustle of leaves in the tall tree ten yards away caught his attention. Riki smiled back at him from between the leaves of a low branch. She hopped to the ground and ran to him.

Nico dropped the basket and caught her in his arms as she entered the camouflaging rows of corn. Hugging her close, he placed little kisses all over her upturned face.

"You scared me, sweetheart."

"I was too afraid to stay in the corn and I figured I could hide in the leafy part of the tree if I was careful."

"Brilliant, Riki. That was good thinking."

She beamed at him and he felt his heart expand. But they were in terrible danger from predators on the ground—both human and not. Nico lifted the basket and led her away from town as quickly and safely as possible, rerouting only once to avoid a large predator eating its nightly kill.

When they were far enough away and out of the corn, Nico stopped.

"I have something for you." He produced the peasant dress with a flourish and was gratified to see tears of happiness in her eyes. She took the dress from him and held it up to her skinny form. "Put it on over what you're wearing for now. It gets cold in the night sky and I want you to be as warm as possible."

Riki tugged the dress on with his help and his breath caught at her beauty. Her gorgeous auburn hair was coming back to life as her energy built with each passing hour of freedom. Riki was beginning to bloom like a flower after long winter, and she was just as enchanting.

A healthy flush lit her pale cheeks. Nico felt better as well after the way their energies fed off each other and multiplied while they slept. He was just glad Riki was starting to regain the health she should have had all along.

"Thank you, Nico!" Riki stretched up to kiss his cheek and the innocent little kiss sang through him. He pulled her into his chest and took her lips with his own, saluting lightly at first, then pushing in with his tongue.

When she didn't resist, he took the kiss deeper—a long, slow exploration of her flavor that drove him nearly wild with desire. Riki clawed at his chest, her hands digging into his muscles, kneading him in a way that made him harder than stone. Warnings shot through his brain. He wanted to ignore the little voice that told him he was taking too much, going too far, but he had to listen. For Riki's sake. Her safety depended on him and he had to put her first.

Nico pulled back, placing soft, nibbling kisses on her full lips.

"You are so beautiful, Riki."

The blush on her cheeks enchanted him. He kissed her softly, mustering all the tenderness he felt for this little, lost princess. Gathering himself, Nico stepped away and lifted the basket once more. He removed a serving of cheese and bread piled together as Riki fussed a bit with her new dress.

"Eat this, for now, and we'll get underway."

Riki did as he asked, silently eating as Nico pulled the length of rope from the basket and set about knotting it just so. Riki watched him quizzically as he worked, but her mouth was full as she chewed and she didn't ask him what he was about. She'd find out soon enough.

Riki was nearly finished with her light meal when Nico swept the black cloak over her shoulders, tucking it up under her chin, glad to see the heavy material enveloped her from head to toe. There were loops and buttons down the front of the well-made cloak and a large hood that could be tied in the upright position. He'd done well with that landlord and Nico would remember the man if they ever made it out of Skithdron.

Buttoning her into the cloak while she finished eating, Nico couldn't help but notice when the backs of his fingers found the swells of her breasts. She gasped, sucking in air as he touched her. Daring greatly, he lingered over the softness of her, allowing his fingers to move slightly from the button between her breasts, experimenting with how far she would let him go.

"Nico—"

He moved back at her breathy protest, though he didn't want to. Still, they were in danger every moment they stayed on the ground. They had to get moving.

"That's for a later time, my lovely." He winked and grinned, enjoying her flushed face in the uncertain light of a crescent moon. "For now, we should be going."

"What's the rope for?" She seemed desperate to change the subject and he let her. For now.

"You'll see," he promised. "You'll have to hold the basket steady, but it'll be worth it when you're hungry. Feel free to eat as we go. I can hunt when we're on the ground, and in dragon form I can eat almost anything, so don't worry about saving anything for me."

"Nico—"

"Don't argue. Come now, we have to go." He moved a short distance away, allowing the change to come over him. *Pick up the rope, sweetheart, and put the large loop over my head.*

He watched understanding dawn over her face. "Won't that be uncomfortable for you?"

No, sweet. But it would make me very uncomfortable *if you were to fall off my back or lose our basket of goodies. Come now, tie it on and let's get moving.*

She complied with only a few murmurs of protest, but he shushed her lovingly and she followed his instructions. Soon he had a harness of sorts around his chest and forearms that would allow her to tie the basket handle—and herself—securely to his back. Riki wasn't an experienced rider and Nico had worried about her safety last night, but had no recourse. This would work, and it would help ease his mind about her safety in the sky just a bit.

Mount up and let's get out of here.

Riki kissed his dragon cheek before doing as he asked, surprising him with the soft gesture. She climbed up on his bent leg and settled against his back with easy familiarity, tying herself to the harness as he'd instructed. A few moments later, he lifted into the air, glad to feel the wind under his wings once more. They were safest in the night sky—at least until they could get out of Skithdron.

Riki wrapped the voluminous cloak around herself, tucking in the edges and securing the hood over her head. It was so beautiful up here in the sky, skidding along with the wisps of cloud and riding so close to the twinkling stars. She'd never forget this experience as long as she lived. The sheer delight of dancing among the stars on a dragon's back was breathtaking and she sat back, simply enjoying the incredible moment of freedom, savoring the peace she had never before known.

How are you doing back there? Nico asked warmly in her mind.

I'm fine, Nico. Just enjoying the night air. It's so exhilarating.

If you get hungry, there's fruit in the basket and more bread and cheese.

Riki was used to hunger pangs, but knew she needed to get her strength back. Reaching into the basket, she pulled out an apple. It had been so long since she'd had fresh, unblemished fruit. The sight of the dark shape in her hand, as they flew through the starlit night, brought tears to her eyes. The past hours were like a dream, but she was living the reality of it. This man—this dragon—and the wonderful, thoughtful gestures he'd made. He was already so special to her. Nico somehow filled her heart with light, and a hope that hadn't been there for many, many years.

Riki? Are you all right?

I'm fine, Nico. Just admiring one of the apples you bought for me. She tried to sound as normal as she could, though her trembling emotions threatened to boil over.

Good. His voice sounded through her mind with a rumble of satisfaction. *I asked the innkeeper to pack his finest and freshest for you. That basket and everything in it is yours, Riki. I want you to eat well and often, to keep your strength up on our journey.*

But what about you? What will you eat?

The dragon beneath her chuckled smokily. *Leave that to me, sweetheart. Dragons are hunters, you know. I'll find game and supply you with fresh meat at the same time. And I can cook it as well.*

Again came the smoky chuckle and she had to laugh too. *You certainly are handy to have around, Nico.*

I'm glad you think so.

They chatted as she munched on the apple and a lovely, ripe pear.

Do you know how far we are from the border?

A day more at least. I'm trying to cut a little northwest, Nico told her as he banked on a gust of wind. She absolutely loved the feeling of flying, being buffeted by the air currents and swimming among the stars. *We have a good chance of connecting with some of the dragons and knights from the Border Lair if we can get close enough. Still, I'm concerned Lucan may have already sent word to the border region and we might find it hard to get across.*

Hard, in what way?

The armies that have attacked Draconia from both the north and east over the past months have been armed with dragon killing weapons. Giant crossbows designed to fling diamond-bladed bolts up into the air. Diamond is about the only thing that can slice through dragon scale with ease. We lost a few dragons during the fighting, and my brother Roland almost died when three bolts hit him. Those weapons are nothing to fool with and they have a lot of them. I'd prefer not to fly anywhere near them if we can help it.

Riki thought back on the many things she'd heard Lucan rant about and some of it began to make sense. *Lucan was supplying Salomar with diamond blades. I remember him saying that more than once.*

Thankfully, Salomar's dead. But you're right about the diamond blades. Salomar used them against our forces when he tried to invade from the north. Your sister was instrumental in foiling his plans. She's quite a woman.

Lana? Riki felt a pang for the girl who had been her other half—torn from her brutally when they'd been stolen from their mother. *Will you tell me about her? What is she doing now?*

Right about now, she's learning how to be Queen of Draconia. She married my brother Roland a few months back.

Lana is the queen?

Yes, sweetheart. And she mother-bonded with a wild Ice Dragon named Tor when he was just hatched from the shell. They've been together ever since. They helped each other escape Salomar and survive in the frozen north until Roland stumbled across their path. He fell in love with Lana almost at first sight, and asked her to be his queen. He adopted Tor and they are raising him together. Tor is an incredibly bright dragonet and can fly amazingly fast and complex patterns.

My sister, the queen. Riki could hardly believe it. *And she lived with a baby dragon?*

You'll love Tor. Kelzy has him calling her grandma.

So my mother is reunited with Kelzy? That's amazing.

Even better, your mother remarried. One of her new husbands is Kelzy's knight partner.

One of her husbands? She has more than one? Riki was a little scandalized by the idea.

It's customary for the knights of fighting dragons to share their mate, since there are so few women who can hear and live with dragons. Plus, the bond between dragon and knight goes so deep, when the dragons come together in passion, so too must the knights with their mate. The knights of mated dragons marry the same woman. Somehow it always seems to work out. The dragons claim the Mother of All guides them in choosing their partners and mates and I have no reason to doubt it. Every marriage I've seen among knights is passionate and happy.

So my mother has two husbands?

Nico chuckled, sending smoke out behind them as they coasted on the air currents. *So does your little sister, Belora. She was the first to marry. One of her knights, Gareth, is partner to Kelzy and Sandor's son, Kelvan.*

So then, Sandor is Kelzy's mate? And if I'm understanding you, Sandor's knight is my mother's other husband?

I think you've got it, sweetheart.

So who is Sandor's knight? What are my step-fathers like?

Sandor's knight is Darian—formerly Lord Darian Vordekrais of Skithdron. He forsook his lands and title to come over to our side and warn us about Lucan and his weapons. He is a hero many times over in Draconia.

I know that name. I heard Lucan rant about Darian. He was so angry, he nearly killed one of his own guardsmen when the news of Lord Darian's defection was reported.

They talked long into the night. Riki was thrilled with the news about her family, surprised by the odd new lifestyle her mother and little sister enjoyed in the Lair, and completely astounded by the idea that her twin was now Queen of Draconia. Nico teased her with funny stories of baby Tor's antics and made her cry with the news that little Belora was going to be a mother at any moment. He was good to talk to and the time passed quickly so she was surprised when the first gray streaks of dawn started showing on the horizon behind them.

He'd told her about her twin sister and the amazing feats of bravery Lana had performed, transforming for the first time into a dragon and flying into the thick of battle to save the king's life. Riki didn't think she'd ever have the nerve to do something so brave. No, Lana was the fearless one. She always had been, and Riki was comforted to know her twin had found a man she could love and who loved her in return.

Still, Riki felt a pang of regret and shame that she had suffered in silence all these years, giving in to Lucan's demands, never once finding a way to escape on her own. Though she had tried repeatedly. Oh, how she'd tried. But failure was her bitter companion. Failure and punishment...and torture.

Riki admired Alania and Belora, and the tales Nico told her of their daring, and her mother's surprising bravery as well. Clinging to a tree with a swarm of skiths below took courage. Nico described how her mother had done that and more. That was the kind of daring Riki feared she would never possess. She felt like such a failure. Such a burden.

She thought of the little she'd managed to accomplish in her life and how often she had failed. Lulled by the morose thoughts, she rested against Nico's warm back. She was snug and warm now, between the woolen cloak and Nico's inner fire. She nearly dozed, but refused to miss a moment of the incredible feeling of flying and seeing the stars so close up. Riki let her gaze drift out and up, pondering the stars, little holes in the fabric of heaven, so near and yet so far.

This doesn't look good. Nico's voice broke into her drifting thoughts.

What? What doesn't look good? Instantly, she was alert. He sounded so serious.

Troop movement. Lots *of troop movement. Lucan's alerted the border garisons.*

How could he inform them so fast?

I didn't want to tell you this, but I heard the guards talking in the tavern. Lucan sent relay riders ahead to the border and every town in between. He wants you back badly enough to put every soldier in this cursed land on alert. They've been riding non-stop since we escaped. When one reaches his destination, another picks up the message and goes to the next stop and so on. Damned efficient and damned inconvenient for us.

What can we do?

Sweetheart, I don't want to risk the border crossing with you on my back. There are limits to how high I can fly safely—especially with a passenger. I can't go high enough to be completely out of range of those diamond blades, and if anything happened to you, I would never forgive myself. It's too risky.

But—

There are other ways, Riki. You have to trust me. I am the Spymaster of Draconia, after all. His sooty laughter was soundless, but she felt the ripples of humor roll through his sinuous neck.

What ways, then?

Well, we could fly northward and try to cross into the Northlands. They might not expect us to try that and the northern border of Skithdron is less heavily fortified than the one with Draconia. Or we could take our chances on the ground for a bit. We'll have to stop soon anyway to rest for the day. My black hide is too easily seen against a light sky.

Do you know where we can go?

I have an idea. There's an operative in place in the city of Plinth. If we can get to him, he might be able to help us.

Operative? What kind of operative are you talking about? A spy?

Actually, by trade, he's a bard. By birth he's Draconian, though you couldn't tell from listening to him. His fathers are knights and he grew up in a Lair, though he struck out on his own at a young age to learn his musical and storytelling craft. He's studied all over and I've always found him helpful. I think his many skills will come in handy now.

I hope you're right.

Chapter Six

And so Nico found himself setting down as gently as he could, just outside the perimeter wall of Plinth a few minutes before dawn. The city was large enough to have a daily market and the gates on the south side were already bustling with traffic as farmers came in from the fields with their sale crops along the large, slightly fortified road. Travel in this part of the country was a little safer than farther south because this far north, the temperatures were colder, meaning fewer skiths inhabited the area.

Nico shifted quickly, lest some sharp-eyed farmer see him in his dragon form. Riki stretched her limbs and Nico was struck for a moment by the lithe grace of her. She swayed from side to side, stretching, Nico thought he'd never seen a more beautiful, feminine sight.

"Is everything all right?"

Nico realized he'd been staring, motionless, for some time. Shaking his head and gathering his wits, he vowed silently to pay better attention to their surroundings. True, he was tired from the long flight and still feeling twinges from the beating and torture he'd suffered just two days before, but that was no excuse for relaxing his vigilance. It wasn't just his life on the line this time. No, Riki was counting on him for protection and guidance through this dangerous land. He couldn't let her down.

"Fine," he answered shortly, stepping closer and straightening the hood on her long traveling cloak. The heavy woolen cloak was a bit large on her, but it wouldn't look too conspicuous in the gray light of dawn and chilly morning air. "We need to blend in with the farmers going to market. Keep the cloak tightly around you, and you should be fine."

He adjusted the hood so it pooled around her face, hiding her a bit. He scooped her auburn hair into a knot, shoving it down the back of the cloak, hiding most of its lustrous length from sight behind the folds of the hood.

"What about you? Won't you look conspicuous in such thin clothes on such a chilly morning?"

Nico stepped back, surveying his work. She looked close to perfect. Or as close to perfect as they could get with such limited resources. His appearance, on the other hand, needed some work before they could blend in. His shirt was burned in places and bloodstained in others. Luckily, the thin, dark leather wasn't very conspicuous in the dim morning light. But they still had to get inside the city and out of public view as quickly as possible.

Rolling back the ragged cuffs of his shirt, Nico adjusted the neckline, tearing into the soft leather, parting it just slightly down his chest and tucking the ragged edges inward. He then took stock of his leather leggings. They'd held up reasonably well through his ordeal, but were clearly worn soldier-style at the moment. Bending, he loosened the hem, pulling on the drawstring he'd had designed right into the garment for just such occasions.

Warriors wore their leathers close so nothing could impede them in battle. Farmers were less particular and usually wore their leather as loose as possible to cool them while they worked, allowing a full range of movement. Farmers were also less apt to be able to afford the custom-made clothes many successful soldiers had tailored from soft, supple leather to address the same range of motion issues. No, loose and hanging out was the order of the day as a farmer, and Nico was prepared.

With a few final tugs, he was ready.

"What do you think?" Nico held his hands out to his sides, sending Riki a smile. She was watching him with such a fierce look of concentration on her cute face, it was all he could do to stop himself from kissing her senseless. Later, he promised himself, when they'd found shelter. Oh, yes, later he'd get that kiss he so desperately needed.

"That's amazing." Riki watched his moves with admiration. He noted the interested spark in her eye as she considered what he'd done to alter his appearance.

Nico bowed slightly with a roguish grin. "If milady will indulge, we must be on our way." He held out one arm and she took it with a silly grin that answered his mood exactly. It was astounding to him how compatible they truly were. Any other woman, by this point in their journey, would have driven him insane with annoyance or boredom, but not Riki. No, the more he got to know her, the more he wanted to know.

They waited for a lull in the traffic to move onto the road, just at the final bend before the city gates. Entering the flow of people, carts and animals as unobtrusively as possible, Nico watched carefully to see if anyone took particular notice of them, but his instincts told him they were safe. For now at least.

They neared the bustling gate area in the dim pre-dawn grayness, little swirls of mist rising about their feet that would burn off when the sun had a chance to peer over the horizon. Riki was a silent shadow at his side, standing straight and steadfast. Still, he was surprised when her little hand fastened itself to his, their fingers intertwining comfortably, as if they belonged together.

The dragon in his soul rose up, growling with satisfaction and he knew it was true. They *did* belong together. Riki was his woman, the partner to his soul. Now he just had to convince her of that fact, though he feared he'd have to move slowly with such a bruised, battered woman.

She was worth it, though. Riki was worth every moment of patience and waiting. Nico knew, eventually, she would be his. And when that day came—when she came to him freely, of her own volition—he would be the luckiest, happiest, most blessed man in the world.

"Morning." Nico nodded nonchalantly to the man standing watch at the gate. The casual greeting and the sureness of his step would go a long way toward forestalling any questions the man might otherwise have about them. Nico swung their clasped hands with a little carefree grin as they passed through the gate without challenge. They gave the appearance of being a young, happy couple, returning from a rendezvous in the fields and after an initial look, no one seemed to notice them.

Just as he'd hoped. So far, so good.

Where are we going? Do you know where your operative is right now? Riki's words echoed silently through his mind, and he was glad she was clever enough to use that ability rather than speaking her fears out loud where anyone might hear. She really was the most astounding woman. For one thing, it was a rare woman indeed who could speak this way with dragonkind.

Rarer still were women of royal blood, with the dragon in their soul. Riki was a treasure.

There is a tavern near the next gate called the Silver Serpent. My man should be there, and if not, we should be able to track him from there easily enough.

What kind of spy is so easy to track? Her voice held confusion and a bit of humor. Riki was proving to be a natural at this kind of thing. Nico put an arm around her shoulders and tucked her close to his side as they continued moving down the lane. It wasn't far now to their destination, which was good because the sun was rising in earnest, soon to be creeping over the walls of the city.

This spy hides in plain sight. As a bard, Drake travels all over, very publicly, with none the wiser to his more clandestine activities.

Amazing.

The little edge of excitement in her thoughts echoed his own love of the profession he'd chosen. Nico had spent a lot of years perfecting his craft in service to the land, people and dragons of Draconia, and his brother Roland, the king.

Turning a corner, Nico spotted the familiar sign. A silver serpent on wooden plaque swung above the door of a moderately successful tavern. Not the best in the city, but far from the worst, this was just the sort of place that would play host to Drake of thc Fivc Lands, bard extraordinaire. While Drake was talented enough to play for kings, he preferred less grand audiences when his time was his own.

Nico knew Drake had just finished a dangerous assignment that took him to the far reaches of Elderland in the east, playing minstrel to the emperor and his court. Having successfully performed his task of foiling an assassination attempt without any of the noble houses of Elderland losing face, Drake had earned the emperor's good favor and a few trade concessions for Draconia as well as some well-deserved time off.

But Drake was never truly at rest. He'd sent word through the usual channels to tell Nico he'd be staying at the Silver Serpent for a few months to see what he might learn of the troubles in Skithdron. Nico thanked the Mother for it now, noting Drake's colorful cart stored half under a tarp in the tavern yard. He was here. Drake of the Five Lands never left his colorful equipage behind. It was as much a part of his persona as his flowing blond hair and winks for the ladies.

Young, old, fat, skinny, short, tall, feisty or docile, Drake loved women of all kinds. And they loved him. Drake had cut a swath through the ladies in all five lands he claimed as his home. Few knew he was really a highly placed son of Draconia, and that alone made him a valuable asset to his true homeland.

This is it. Nico pulled Riki closer into his side, shielding her from the single large window into the taproom by placing himself between her and it. *We're in luck. See that blue wagon under the cloth over there? That's Drake's wagon. Which means he's in residence.*

Nico noted the subtle way she looked to the wagon. This remarkable woman was a natural at the spy game, did she but know it.

And you think he'll help us?

I know he will.

You trust this man? Fear laced her tone and he squeezed her gently as he met her gaze.

With my life.

Nico walked past the main entrance of the tavern, knowing Drake wouldn't be up and about in the main rooms yet. It was too early for a man who played late into the night to be awake, for one thing. For another, Drake wasn't on assignment, which meant his time was his own. No doubt he was with one of his many legions of women and had spent most of the night in pleasure.

Aren't we going in? Riki asked quietly in his mind, though her steps didn't falter. She followed where he led, giving him a surprising sense of satisfaction.

Not by the front door. There's a smaller entrance 'round the back. Drake's room should be near there, but we'll wait for his signal before going inside. Just be as quiet as you can and follow my lead.

Of course, Nico. You've gotten us this far.

Her warm tone filled him with unexpected pride that she would place such trust in him on such short acquaintance. Of course, his dragon soul knew her—and wanted her—but he couldn't be as sure of what she felt. This little indication of trust was all the more touching because of it.

But he couldn't let himself be distracted. This was a crucial moment. They couldn't be seen loitering around the back alleys, but they also couldn't just barge into the tavern making a grand entrance. This had to be done with finesse.

Walking nonchalantly around back, Nico eyed the surroundings with subtle interest. No one was about, which was a relief. Quietly he positioned himself near the back door, leaning against a support and tugging Riki into his arms.

In case anyone is watching, we're just two lovers out for a quick cuddle before we go in.

Riki smiled up at him with utter trust and Nico bent down to kiss her sweet lips just once. He couldn't afford the more leisurely exploration he really wanted. They just didn't have time. Nico had to get her inside before the sun rose above the city walls and anyone could see the state of their clothing in the full light of day. That would be remarked upon, and if anyone started asking, they'd be fingered for certain.

Stay right there, sweetheart. Nico pulled her against him, settling his cheek against hers just enough to hide the lower part of his face in the folds of the hood, which was resting in bunches around her shoulders. Pursing his lips, he gave the soft call of a dove. Altered just slightly, this particular call should alert Drake to their presence.

Nico nuzzled Riki's neck as he waited, his muscles bunched with tension until he felt her fingers rubbing circles on his straining shoulders. He was about to give the call again when the back door opened and Drake's unmistakable blond hair shone bright in the dim light as he leaned out.

Nico straightened casually and took Riki's hand. *Let's go. Just move quietly, like we belong here, and all should be well.*

Is that your operative?

Yes, that's him. He's a good friend as well, so I know we'll be safe with him, Riki. You have nothing to fear from him. You can trust me on this.

I do, Nico.

He squeezed her hand as they strolled past Drake into the sleepy tavern. Only a few people were stirring in the kitchen. Nico could hear the motions of cooking and smell the beginnings of breakfast from the far side of the hall as Drake motioned them into the doorway closest to the back door. Nico smiled at the good placement. Drake wasn't one of his best operatives for nothing.

As soon as the door closed behind them, Nico turned to his friend.

"What? No female companionship last night?" He made a tsking sound as he shook his head, speaking softly, wary of the thin walls and possibility of listening ears around them. "Drake, you shock me."

But Drake wasn't laughing. He spoke in low tones as well. "I heard about your capture just last night from the scoundrel who sold you out. He's been dealt with." The grim set to his mouth assured Nico the man wouldn't be double crossing anyone ever again. "I'd planned to head south today, to see if I could be of assistance, then I find you at my doorstep. And with a lovely companion, no less."

No doubt Drake was being cautious around Riki. He didn't know who or what she was, after all. Nico relished the moment, knowing how surprised Drake would be when he learned their quest for the new queen's sister was at an end.

Nico drew Riki forward to face Drake. "Sweetheart," he addressed her softly, "may I present Drake of the Five Lands."

"Bard extraordinaire," Drake added with a twinkling smile. "He always forgets that part."

Riki chuckled, the sound enchanting Nico as he continued the introductions.

"Drake, this is Riki. The one we've all been searching for."

Nico felt satisfaction as Drake's eyes widened. Drake looked back at Riki, clearly astounded to realize just who she was.

"Are you certain?" Drake whispered.

Nico nodded. "She healed me." He knew that was all the proof Drake would need. He was one of the few who knew the secrets of royal blood.

Drake dropped to one knee before them. "Thank the Mother for your return, milady."

Riki squirmed as the tall blond man knelt before her. No one had ever seemed so pleased to see her—not counting Nico's initial reactions, of course. If this was the kind of reception she was going to get in Draconia, she would be forever blushing. As she was sure her face was flaming at that very moment.

"Um...I'm pleased to meet you, sir."

The blond man's gaze went from her to Nico with apparent amusement.

"Get up, you fool," Nico chastised the man with good humor. It was clear to her these men were long-time friends from the easy way they conversed. "You're making the poor girl blush."

She just *knew* it. Could she be any more embarrassed?

Drake got to his feet, taking her free hand in his on the way up and dragging it to his lips for a kiss. Nico's grip tightened on her other hand and pulled her back toward him as he growled low in his throat.

"She's not here for your amusement, Drake." Nico's tone excited her. He sounded almost...possessive.

Drake winked at her and let her hand go gently. "How can I help?"

"We need food and sleep. We flew all night."

"Can she—?"

Riki got the impression he was asking if she could shift into dragon form, but that would mean he knew about her sister. Then again, he was a highly placed spy and apparently a good friend of Nico's. It was more than likely he did know, and she felt suddenly self-conscious as Nico shook his head negatively, cutting off that line of inquiry. She felt somehow...less...because she couldn't do what Lana apparently could. She couldn't turn into a dragon and she couldn't have escaped on her own like Lana did. All in all, she was falling far short of Lana's accomplishments and though she loved her sister dearly, she felt sorry for herself.

"Can you get some food for us without raising suspicion?" Nico asked quietly, redirecting the conversation.

"We still have a few things in the basket." Riki raised an arm, over which the handle of the basket still rested. It was lighter now, to be sure, but she had managed to save some of the fruit for Nico.

"It's no problem," Drake said softly, "I often eat in with my...uh...guests. Eyebrows will not be raised by a large breakfast order coming from me."

"Then perhaps we could arrange to 'arrive' as your cousins later this evening after we've rested and you can get some provisions for us."

Drake nodded, his eyes serious. "I'll make the purchases today. I assume you lost everything when you were captured?"

Nico nodded. "Riki needs clothes as well."

"You sly devil." Drake winked outrageously at her as she chuckled once more. Oh, he was a charming rogue and totally out of her experience.

"Knock it off, Drake." Nico tugged her back against his chest, one arm banding around her waist. Riki practically purred as Nico staked such a public claim. She had no idea if he meant it for keeps or as just a way to keep her safe from Drake, but she liked it, to be certain. "She's been held captive for years. She has nothing of her own. I want you to get as much as you can for her in the market. She deserves to be spoiled a little. At least as much as we can manage on such short notice."

"Heard and understood, boss." Drake's eyes lit with sympathy and she wasn't above accepting it right now. She'd been through a lot and would most likely fall asleep in a heap on the floor if Nico wasn't holding her up. It had been a long few days since escaping the palace, but the time with Nico had been the most exhilarating, if the most exhausting, of her life thus far.

"I'll just nip down to the kitchen and ask Themla to make up a tray." Drake turned toward the door, but paused, looking back at Nico first, then at her, his expression clouded. "I'm glad you're safe."

Riki sensed the very deep feeling in the handsome man's quiet words. She knew they were meant for Nico and the slight tightening of his arm at her waist told her how deeply Drake's words were felt in return.

"Me too, my friend. Me too."

Drake left then, and Nico let her go when she pulled slightly against his hold. Turning in a circle, she got a chance to look over the small, but neat room. There was a large bed in one corner that looked like heaven itself to her. Even rumpled from having been slept in by the blond giant, the mattress looked soft and inviting. Riki hadn't slept in a real bed in years. Though she'd been chained at times to Lucan's, she had never even been tempted to sit on the edge of that vile piece of furniture when he wasn't around.

Anything Lucan touched was contaminated as far as she was concerned and she far preferred the hard marble floor to sleep on than anything he would give her. Of course, he never once offered even a thin mat for her comfort. She was there for his comfort alone—no one else's—and the point was driven home by all the little slights and inconveniences as well as the beatings and screaming threats.

But it was all behind her now. And Drake's bed was before her.

"There's a chamber pot behind the screen, if you need it," Nico said from behind her. She started, waking from her dazed thoughts. She was quite literally asleep on her feet. "Or you could just lie down. You look done in, sweetheart. Why don't you go to sleep?"

Riki couldn't resist the temptation the bed represented. Stumbling a little as she moved forward, she had only the presence of mind to unbutton the cloak and allow it and the basket to slide off her arms just before she reached the bed. Collapsing on it face down, she felt Nico tug the thin blanket up over her, settling her more comfortably.

She made an effort to turn onto her side so she could see him. Surprisingly, he was bending over to collect and fold the cloak, putting it over the foot of the bed, giving extra warmth to her cold feet. Riki smiled up at him.

"I'm sorry. I can't seem to keep my eyes open."

Nico chuckled. "It's all right, sweetheart." He sat on the side of the bed, leaning over her a little to kiss her brow. "Go to sleep. There will be food here when you wake and I won't leave you for one moment."

"Do you promise?" She yawned as sleep threatened to claim her.

"I do, my love. I'll watch over you and protect you all the days of my life."

Riki couldn't be certain later if Nico actually spoke the words or if she just dreamed them. Ah, but what a beautiful dream.

Chapter Seven

Drake pushed open the door some moments later, holding a large tray before him. Nico met him at the door, took the tray and deposited it on the room's only table. Nico sat down and dug into the hot oatmeal, knowing it wouldn't keep while Riki slept. He'd leave the bread and jams for her, as well as some of the fruit and cheese, but the fried eggs and bacon, as well as the oatmeal, was his.

The important thing was, they could get more. Drake would hide them and keep them as safe as possible while they were with him. Though he didn't see Drake much nowadays, they'd been raised together, trained together as soldiers and in their lessons. They were close friends and Nico trusted Drake with his life—and now with Riki's life as well.

"She asleep?" Drake asked quietly, nodding toward the bed.

Nico nodded. "The journey's been rough on her, and she was in bad shape when I found her. Lucan beat and starved her for the past year or more, from what I can tell. He had her chained to his bed."

Drake's eyes narrowed. "He hurt her?"

"Not the way you think." Nico was quick to correct the assumption, though his voice was grim. "For some reason, Loralie the witch told Lucan that Riki would lose her healing power if she wasn't a virgin. It's the only thing that's protected her from rape, but he's hurt her in other ways." Nico's blood ran hot with anger as he thought what Riki must have suffered.

"She's special to you, isn't she?" Drake's eyes softened as he looked at the sleeping woman.

"She's the one, Drake."

"Does she know that yet?" Drake looked speculative, and more than a little shocked, but Drake had grown up in a Lair. Drake was well aware of how quickly knights and dragons knew when they'd met the one woman meant for them. Dragons and knights both had very strong bonds with their chosen mates, and Nico was a little of both.

Nico shook his head, his gaze focused on Riki, sleeping soundly, nearly swallowed up by the big bed. "With what she's been through, I'm surprised she's even still sane. Lucan's not quite human anymore, Drake."

"I'd heard rumors."

"I've seen it firsthand." Nico eyed his old friend, driving home the urgency of his words. "According to Riki, Lucan made a deal with Salomar. He traded diamond blades and an alliance against us, in return for use of Salomar's pet witch, Loralie." Nico resumed eating as he related the details Riki had given him about how the North Witch had blended Lucan with the skiths, mingling their blood with his in painful treatments Riki had witnessed. It had been her duty to heal the tyrant after the treatments, weakening herself in the process.

"Lucan kept her starved and weak and when she didn't comply with his demands, he beat her bloody. There are scars all over her body and you can see how thin she is. She looked even worse two days ago." Anger rose as Nico spoke, but he was careful to keep control of the seething dragon within.

"The poor mite." Drake's expression was filled with pity as he watched Riki sleep. Nico felt possessive of her, but there was also a sense of thankfulness that his friend would feel protective of her too. Drake was fiercely loyal and had a soft heart he tried hard to hide, but Nico had known him since they were both boys. Their bonds ran deep.

"She's got fire, Drake, and spirit. Lucan wasn't able to crush it out of her, but she's unsure of herself. She has little sense of her own self-worth. We must tread lightly with her feelings."

"Which is why, I take it, you're giving her time."

"She's the most precious thing in my world, Drake. She can have all the time she needs."

"Well," Drake stood from the table, "things will be easier once we get you out of Skithdron. I'm going to the market to get your supplies and talk to a few friends. Unless there's trouble, I'll return just before sundown. The common room of the tavern doesn't start filling up until dinnertime, which starts one mark after sundown in these parts. You can 'arrive' during the dinner bustle with none the wiser."

"A good plan." Nico rose and held his hand out to Drake in the warrior's way. They clasped, giving each other a brief clap on the back, another indication of their closeness. "You're a good friend, Drake. I'm putting not just my safety, but that of my mate in your hands."

Drake sent one last look over at the sleeping woman, his expression softer than Nico had ever seen it. "I won't let you down."

"I know, Drake. That's why I came to you. There are precious few men I would trust in this world. You've always been top on the list."

Drake bowed his head briefly. "I'm honored."

Nico secured the bolt after Drake left without making a sound. He surveyed the room. The leftover food on the big tray would make a good meal for Riki, whenever she woke. Nico's own hunger was satisfied for the time being.

Well, at least his hunger for *food* was satisfied. His hunger for Riki was something he was discovering was a constant. It didn't matter where they were or in what kind of situation. He always hungered for her. It was fast becoming part of his nature, and he knew it would only grow worse the more time he spent with her.

Personally, he didn't care. Nico wanted the closeness. He wanted the bond. He wanted her. Period.

If he had to wait, so be it. Riki was worth every effort, every sacrifice, every moment of his time. She was his love. It was just that simple.

And that devastating.

Shucking his shirt and boots, Nico lay down next to her on the large bed. He decided to keep his leggings on. First, because they were in a strange city in a strange bed and he might need to jump into action quickly should something go wrong. Second, he didn't quite trust himself not to take Riki's soft body with his, even in sleep, if there were no barrier between them. It was safer to have at least one or two layers of cloth between them. At least until they settled things and Riki became his lover, mate, and wife.

With a hearty sigh, Nico put his arm around Riki's waist and pulled her unresisting body back against his own. She settled into the curve of him as if she belonged there and he felt a great sense of satisfaction.

Finally, he slept, cradling the woman he loved in his arms.

Riki woke feeling warm and comforted, and incredibly aroused. She was lying on a cloud—which she came to realize was really Drake's borrowed bed, as her senses began to clear.

Nico had her wrapped deep in his arms, and his hands were under her dress, which had been pulled up around her waist under cover of the warm blankets. His chest heated her back, his strong arms encasing her in warmth, his hand plying one nipple and the other resting at the juncture of her thighs.

No other man had ever touched her so tenderly, so hotly, so enticingly. Only Nico.

She tried to turn in his arms, but he stilled her.

"Ssh, sweetheart. Just lie back and enjoy." His strong fingers lifted her thigh, moving her leg over his as he tangled them together. She felt the soft leather of his leggings rubbing between her thighs with a sense of wonder. It felt so good!

But what he did next felt even better. Nico's hand moved, his fingers searching among her folds and finding a little nubbin of flesh that seemed connected directly with her womb. As he stroked it, she felt her insides quiver and the dampness of excitement flow from her core. Nico rubbed his bristly chin against the back of her neck and nipped lightly, sending shivers down her spine.

She felt him smile against her neck as his fingers slid in the wetness between her legs. She tried to pull back, embarrassed, but he would have none of it. His strong arms held her steady, his legs pinioning hers.

"You're so wet for me, my dove, so eager for my touch. Do you know how much that means to me? Do you know how much you excite me?"

Nico pushed his hips against hers and she felt the hard rod of his erection against her backside, through the soft leather of his leggings. He was well endowed and very ready.

But she wasn't. She feared she would never be ready to give up her virginity—not while the threat of Lucan loomed over her head.

Riki pulled back and this time Nico let her move away just slightly, though his hands still roamed over her body. His hand at her breast tugged and teased the nipple, sending lightning bolts down to her core. The hand between her thighs played with the little bud, moving lower to slide in her juices, then dipping within her tight channel. One long finger slid into her, stretching her, filling her. It felt so wonderful, so strange, so full. She wanted more, but she knew she couldn't indulge. Even this was dangerous.

She whimpered as he began to move in and out, that single finger teasing her virgin channel, the rest of his hand grinding against the little button that brought such pleasure. She squirmed to get closer, to get away, to just get something. She didn't know what. But she needed something that only Nico could provide.

"Please!" she whispered, arching back against him.

"Come for me, sweetheart, let it all go. Trust in me, trust in this. Come for me now." His whispered words slid into her ear, followed by his tongue a moment later, driving the fire higher and hotter still.

Nico moved lower and bit down on her neck, the savage action spurring her to the greatest heights yet as his hands continued their skillful seduction of her senses. With a little cry, she crept up and over some unknown precipice, but Nico was there to catch her as the orgasm broke over her trembling, yearning body.

She felt like she was floating, free-falling down from a very high mountain peak. Nico continued to stroke her, and guide her, throughout. He was such a good, strong, dear man. And now he'd shown her the most incredible feelings. How could she continue to deny herself—deny them—this pleasure, this passion?

"Nico?"

"Ssh, my sweet, just relax. Sleep a bit more if you can. Drake will be back soon with some new clothes for you."

"But what about you?"

"Don't worry about me, Riki. You come first. Always. Sleep now." He stroked back her hair and she could feel the tension in his body.

Riki tried to close her eyes and go to sleep but couldn't, knowing he was suffering because of her. She knew enough about men's bodies— from having been subjected to watching Lucan and his lovers of both sexes—to know Nico needed relief. Gathering her courage, she turned in his arms, sitting up slightly so she could look into his lovely hazel eyes.

"My body may be virgin, Nico, and I need to keep it that way for now, but I know you need me. I can't give you my virginity, but I can give you relief."

"No, sweetheart," Nico tried to push her gently away as she lowered the blanket and set to work on the ties that held his leggings in place, but she would not be deterred.

She looked up at him with a self-conscious smile. "You know, I've never done this before."

"Lucan never made you—"

"No. He made me watch, but Loralie told him to leave me alone sexually in every way. I have that to thank her for, I suppose, though she's the one who brought my healing gift to his attention in the first place." She paused as he breathed a sigh of relief. "I've been curious about some of the things I saw."

"Lucan is a monster, Riki. Some of the things you saw—"

"Oh, I know some of that was the result of a sick mind, but other things...back in the beginning, when he was still mostly human...those things I've been curious about."

"Such as?" Nico raised one eyebrow in her direction and she knew he would let her try whatever she liked. She smiled at him.

"I want to taste you, Nico. I want to know what you feel like in my mouth. Will you let me do that?"

"Sweet Mother." Nico's head dropped back as she unlaced his leggings. "I don't know if I'll survive this, but do what you want, angel. Whatever you want."

She gasped as his hard cock sprang out of the confining leather and into her hand. He was warm and solid, and so big. None of the men she'd seen in Lucan's chambers could compare to the length and width of Nico. She was almost afraid he wouldn't fit in her mouth, but she'd do her best.

"Tell me if I do anything wrong. I don't want to hurt you, Nico."

She stroked her hands around him, lowering the leggings a little farther so she could cup his balls in one questing hand. He was so perfectly formed, so incredibly beautiful.

"Sweetheart, you couldn't hurt me if you tried. Anything you do pleases me. Anything." She squeezed him experimentally with her hand. "Oh yeah." He groaned as his head dropped back once more.

Encouraged by his response, Riki bent her head and licked at the head of his cock, learning his taste little by little. He tasted good and smelled even better—musky, warm and faintly of exotic cinnamon. She licked him like a stick of candy, running her tongue up his shaft more boldly now as he clutched the blankets on either side.

Daring greatly, she sank down onto him, opening her mouth wide, trying to take as much of him as she could, all the way to the back of her throat. She just wanted to see if she could and was pleasantly surprised by both the tensing of his muscles and the low growls coming from deep in his chest. The sleeping dragon had been awakened, she thought with an inward smile.

Sucking her cheeks hollow, she lifted up, not letting him go completely, but moving on him with hesitant motions. Riki grew bolder as Nico's excitement increased, loving the way he responded to the lightest touch of her tongue.

"Come up here, sweetheart."

Nico surprised her when his strong hand found her knee, coaxing her to move around on the bed until she was kneeling, parallel to his body. She nearly fainted when he flipped the dress up over her hips, his warm hand settling over her pussy with knowing, sure moves. Riki would have objected, but her mouth was full of Nico. And then objections were forgotten as Nico stroked her passion higher with those wicked fingers of his. She moaned around his cock.

"Oh, baby. Just like that." He put one hand in her hair, almost guiding her head in its up and down motions as his other hand toyed with her pussy. Riki felt her own excitement growing with every stroke of his hand, every pulsing lick of her tongue on his hard shaft.

The pressure rose, higher and higher, while he stroked one long finger in and out of her virgin hole. His hand rubbed all over, bringing her back to that peak of excitement she had just learned at his hands. Riki sucked him harder, loving the salty, sweet taste of him on her tongue. She wanted to please him. She wanted to give him the greatest pleasure he'd ever known. She wanted all of him. If only for this moment.

"Baby, I'm going to come," he warned her, trying to pull her up and off him, but she wasn't going anywhere. She wanted it all.

Nico came with a muffled shout that spurred her own excitement higher as she swallowed everything he gave her. This was so special, so magical, so good. This just felt right as nothing in her life ever had before.

Nico groaned as he came in Riki's hot mouth. For a novice, she was a natural at sucking cock and it didn't take much for him to lose all semblance of control. She was downright dangerous.

Riki swallowed every last drop of his cum, then licked him clean with her clever tongue, very nearly making him hard all over again. But he couldn't afford that. With smooth motions, he sat up and lifted her by the waist, plunking her down on the bed beneath him. She was breathing fast, her pussy swollen and weeping with excitement as he spread her legs, the juncture of her thighs open to his hungry gaze.

"Nico, I can't." Her shocked whisper brought his eyes up to hers.

"I won't take your virginity until you beg me, Riki. That's a promise. But I will eat your pussy, like you just sucked my cock. Stars, baby! You nearly blinded me with pleasure." He dropped down over her, fitting his bare cock against the sweet wet spot between her thighs and rubbing as he kissed her lips and delved into her mouth. She was hot and sultry, and she tasted faintly of him, which was incredibly arousing.

Kissing her deeply, as if he wanted to devour her, he rubbed all over her beautiful body. The dress was up around her waist and Nico took a moment to push it higher still, so he could feel her soft breasts against his chest. He blanketed her, wishing he could take this to its ultimate conclusion, but knowing, for her sake, he couldn't…yet.

"Nico!" Her breathy whisper near his ear told him she was nearing a peak, but he didn't want her coming until he'd had a chance to taste her cream.

"Hold on, baby. Just a little bit longer. I want to lick you the way you just licked me."

Her little body shuddered under him as he rolled down the bed, kissing, licking and nibbling her skin as he went. He paused at her breasts, sucking the hard nipples into his mouth, laving them with his tongue, one by one. She squirmed under him in a most satisfying way as he continued down her body, teasing her belly button and nibbling the bones of her hips. She was still much too thin, but he would do something about that, given time. He would feed her the finest foods in the land, shower her with delicacies from every corner of the world, if it would make her as healthy as she should be.

Moving lower, he spread her pussy open with his fingers and just looked for a long moment. The puffy pink paradise called to him, but he took a moment to savor his first clear sight of her most private place. He knew he was the first man to show her the pleasure of her body, and he relished the thought, but he was dying to be inside her and knew that would come only when—and if—she wanted it.

Until then, he would have to satisfy himself with this. But this was a heaven of a different sort, and no less sweet. Nico bent to his task with relish, licking his way around her pussy, learning her taste and her responses. Delicately he nipped at her nether lips, teasing and tasting until he found her sensitive clit. She cried out softly when he sucked her there, losing it completely when he slid his middle finger into her responsive core and stroked carefully.

She came apart for him, biting back her cries in an effort to keep the noise level down. Oh, what he wouldn't give to hear her scream in pleasure and cry out his name.

Nico heard the door open, but one quick look up told him it was only Drake. The other man looked shocked for a moment, and then a grin spread across his face.

"I could come back later, if you like."

Riki gasped and tried to push away, but Nico only smiled.

"Get in and close the door, Drake. I was just showing my woman how much I appreciate her."

Drake smiled with wicked enjoyment, winking at Riki to help ease her embarrassment at being caught. "If she were mine, I'd do the same, Nick. Night and day. You're a lucky, lucky man."

Riki finally found the strength to pull down the dress, at least over her breasts, but Nico still sat firmly between her thighs, keeping them spread. Riki wasn't reacting as violently as he thought she would. Could it be she liked being watched? Did she have that little bit of the exhibitionist in her?

Most dragons did, Nico well knew. Mating flights tended to be flagrantly public affairs and the dragon in him thrilled to the idea of having everyone witness his joining with his mate. He remembered how Roland and Lana had reveled in their lovemaking in dragon form and in private. It stood to reason that as Riki's dragon side awoke, so too would her own daring and desire for a little sexual exhibitionism.

Testing her, Nico spread her pussy wide, examining it fully before bending to place a few little biting kisses on her clit. Riki fairly jumped off the bed as her pussy flooded with a fresh wave of telling cream.

"Will you look at that?" Drake drawled, clearly at ease with the situation. "I think she likes you."

"No doubt about it," Nico agreed, sitting back a little and letting Drake look his fill. Nico watched Riki's eyes and the reactions of her body as Drake moved closer. Damn, if his little woman wasn't excited by the other man's eyes on her naked pussy. He thought to push her one step further. "Hold her hands while I lick her clean. I think she needs to come once more for me before I'll be satisfied."

Drake approached quietly, sitting at the side of the bed and taking Riki's fragile wrists into one of his big hands. He held them loosely, but firmly, up above her head.

"Is this all right?" Drake asked. Nico was proud of her when she nodded. Her cheeks were flushed, probably with a mix of both embarrassment and excitement if he were any judge, but she was definitely responding to Nico's desires, pushing the limits of her comfort zone.

"She has pretty tits," Nico pushed a bit further, step by step.

"Really?" Drake asked dryly, obviously waiting to see where this would all lead.

"Can we show Drake your tits, baby? Will you let him play with your nipples while I stick my tongue up your pussy?"

Riki gasped, but nodded shyly, her luminous green eyes going wide as Nico lifted her dress up and over her shoulders, baring her completely. The dress tangled around her wrists, effectively binding her hands, which was all to the good when Drake reached down with both hands to fondle her breasts.

Nico took her shiver as a sign she was nearing another peak. He wanted his tongue inside her this time when she flew. It was the closest he could come at this point to possessing her completely, and it would have to do for now. Dropping down, Nico held her gaze while he zeroed in on her clit with his tongue and gentle nips of his teeth.

"You're right, Nick, your girl has very pretty titties. Do you think she'd let me kiss them?"

"Pushing it, don't you think, Drake?" Nico asked as he rose up just a little from his assault on her clit. But then Nico felt the jump in her pulse and the excitement in her eyes and he relented. He would give Riki anything she desired. Anything. "Go ahead, Drake. Taste her nipples. They're the finest in the land."

"No doubt," Drake smiled as he leaned down, blocking Nico's view of Riki's eyes, but it was all right. He felt her in his heart, in his soul. He knew she was enjoying this journey of discovery as much as he was. He resumed licking her pussy, laving up every drop of her cream and fucking in and out of her with his tongue while his slick fingers dropped down even lower to tease the forbidden hole at the back of her body.

Riki jumped when he inserted his finger just a short distance into her ass, but didn't demure. No, his girl was with him every step of the way.

Chapter Eight

Riki couldn't believe what was happening. Nico was thrusting his tongue in and out, driving her wild, while his devilish friend nibbled on her nipples. She'd never felt so wanton—or so excited—in her entire life. Admittedly, her experience was nil, but she'd seen all manner of things in Lucan's rooms. This, by far, was the most exciting.

Drake stared deep into her eyes as he lifted up just slightly, tugging at one nipple with the barest graze of his teeth. His blue eyes flashed so brightly, they reminded her of the precious blue gems in some of Lucan's crown jewels. Sapphires, she thought they were called. Drake's sapphire eyes were filled with devilish amusement, daring her to join in the fun.

But her senses were completely overwhelmed by Nico's skillful tongue working its magic below. With a whimpering cry, she came hard against his tongue, flying higher than she had before, soaring above the earth as she experienced the greatest pleasure she'd felt yet under Nico's skillful direction. He licked her and sucked lightly throughout, holding her at the pinnacle for a timeless moment, stretching the pleasure out.

When she finally settled back to earth, Drake was watching her, his handsome face mere inches from her own, his smile wide and genuine.

"I thank you, milady."

"Um," she spoke softly, embarrassment flooding her cheeks with heat, "I think that should be the other way around."

Drake chuckled as Nico finally rose from between her legs, peering over Drake's shoulder as he caressed her thighs with his big hands, soothing her. She liked the way he watched over her, caring for her safety and pleasure above his own.

Drake moved down and Nico growled. But Drake only shrugged as he placed a light kiss on Riki's lips, a soft salutation of friendship and respect. She felt all that in his kiss, just as she felt Nico's possessive grip on her thighs tighten until Drake moved back, rising to his feet beside the bed. He moved casually to the things he'd dropped on the table and chair by the door and Riki took a moment to catch her breath. There was still Nico to deal with and she could feel him staring at her naked form.

She couldn't quite meet his eyes yet and like a coward, she shut her own, hiding. It took her by surprise when she felt Nico kiss the small scar on her waist—the deepest one among many from Lucan's skith venom torture sessions. She knew the wound was ugly and tears came to her eyes when she felt Nico kiss each and every one of her scars on his way up her body. At length, he settled over her, blanketing her with his warm length.

"Look at me, sweetheart."

"I can't."

"You must." His voice cajoled, teasing her into doing his bidding. "Or we will lie like this all night and in such case, I cannot guarantee you will wake a virgin."

"Nico!" She gasped at his blatant teasing, knowing Drake could hear everything, and opened her eyes directly into Nico's hazel gaze.

He was smiling so beautifully, she felt it in her knees. He really was the most handsome man she had ever set eyes on. And the most giving.

"Drake knows, sweetheart. He knows how you've been treated, and he will protect you, just as I will."

"I trust you, Nico." Her words seemed to affect him greatly. His jaw clenched and something like hope burst in his gaze, only to be tamped down as he rolled slightly away.

"Are you all right with what just happened?"

Riki ducked her head, embarrassed to talk so openly about the scandalous things she'd just let them do to her body. But Nico tipped her chin up, forcing her gaze to meet his.

"Don't hide, sweetheart. I didn't mean to rush you, but you were so sweetly responsive in my arms, I couldn't help myself. It's perfectly normal to enjoy what we did. I only regret if I pushed you too far. Did you enjoy it?"

"You know I did." The admission was forced from the depths of her embarrassment.

Nico beamed and kissed her deeply, rubbing himself lightly against her. When he let her up for air, she was panting once more. The man was potent.

"Good. You've made me very happy, Riki. Thank you."

She knew he was talking about her daring actions before Drake arrived and she was glad Nico didn't go into specifics with the other man present, no matter what they had just shared. Some things were meant to be private, between herself and Nico alone.

"You're welcome."

Drake laughed from the corner of the room. "You two are more formal than my granny."

Nico threw a pillow at Drake, but levered himself up from the bed, tugging at his leggings as he went, covering himself. Riki felt a pang of regret when he was all tucked away. With some shock, she realized she actually wanted to see a man's cock, wanted to lick it, wanted to own it.

But there was work to be done.

Riki watched Nico saunter over to the table, picking up the sword Drake placed before him. Expertly, he tested the balance as Riki scrambled to a sitting position on the bed, tugging her dress down over her body and pulling a blanket around her shoulders for good measure. She wasn't normally comfortable showing her body because of all the scars. The minutes before had been an aberration caused by extreme pleasure. Pleasure so intense, her cheeks flooded with heat, and her pussy with cream, just remembering it.

Nico inhaled deeply and turned to wink at her. His smile was downright wicked. Riki began to wonder just how acute dragon senses were. Could he actually smell her renewed arousal? It certainly seemed as if he could.

"This is a fine blade," Nico nodded at Drake. "Good choice."

Drake nodded, passing a set of knives to Nico. "Try these. There's a fairly good swordsmith in town, willing to work quietly and not ask any questions."

"Ah, the best kind," Nico agreed, testing the weight of each of the blades with a critical eye. "These are fine too. Your smith is a good one. Did you manage to get anything for Riki?"

Drake grinned broadly and with a flourish, produced a bright red dress with yellow trim and enough frills to make Riki blink twice. It had a wide, tiered skirt, and a neckline that would scoop low over her breasts, but the sleeves would probably come all the way to the middle of her forearms, hiding the worst of her scars and providing some warmth. It was flamboyant, but beautiful, and Riki could barely believe it was meant for her.

Nico took it from Drake with gentle hands and walked over to the bed, sitting at her side. He draped the dress over her legs. “I want you to wear this, sweetheart. I know it’s a little bright, but we’re posing as Drake’s cousins from the Jinn. Most of the Jinn women dress in very bright colors and it will help to camouflage you.”

It touched her that he would worry over whether she liked the dress or not, but he didn’t truly understand her apprehension. Somehow, she needed to make him understand.

“It’s a beautiful dress, Nico,” she said softly. “Neither the color nor style bothers me. It’s just...I’ve never worn something so pretty. Or so new.”

Nico reached out and pulled her into his arms, rocking her close to his solid chest. “You will have rooms of new dresses and gowns when I get you home to Draconia. I’ll see to it myself. Nothing is too good for you, Riki.” His fervently whispered words brought tears to her eyes as he rocked her ever so gently. “Put on the dress, sweetheart. Let’s begin your new life with this small step.”

He pulled back slowly and unwrapped the blanket from her shoulders. She let him. Tugging her old dress up, he pulled it over her head, but the light in his eyes was only partly sexual. No, his heat was tempered with care, gentleness and something she couldn’t quite name, but the flavor of it humbled her. Holding her gaze, Nico dropped the new dress over her head and tugged it down over her breasts and against her waist.

“Stand up, sweetheart.” Gingerly, she got to her feet at the side of the bed, allowing the material to swish down around her legs. The dress fell nearly all the way to the floor, swirling around her ankles, delicate as moth’s wings. Nico moved behind her to tie the sash that would fit the dress around her waist snugly and for the first time in her life, Riki felt feminine and pretty in the soft red dress. She spun and the voluminous, light skirt trailed a few seconds behind her movement. Experimentally, she tried moving a bit more and delighted in the swish of the silky material.

"It's so beautiful."

"*You're* beautiful," Nico breathed, watching her. Her eyes flew to his and she read hunger in his gaze—hunger and admiration that set her knees to wobbling.

"I agree." Drake spoke from behind her, breaking the spell. "You look like a Jinn princess. It's a perfect disguise. All it needs is this around your beautiful hair." Drake produced a matching red, patterned scarf with lovely long fringe all around. He moved close to place it in her hand and Riki sighed at the whisper soft material that met her touch. "Silk, from the eastern shores, for the Jinn princess, and golden bangles for your arms." Drake produced three gold bracelets and held them up before her with a devilish smile.

"They're perfect, Drake." Nico stepped forward to examine the jewelry, holding out his hands for more. "What else did you get?"

Drake handed Nico a few other items but Riki couldn't see what they were and she was too entranced by her new dress to really care. The men were the experts at this spy game, she was just a new player who must work hard to keep up.

Nico turned and captured her hand, surprising her for a moment. Gently, he slid the bangles onto her arms, then placed a plain gold band around her finger, holding her gaze all the while. She knew in some lands, such rings were meant as mating gifts and it touched her that he would place such a mark on her finger. She noticed then, looking down to admire the ring, that he wore a matching band on his own finger.

"We're mated," he said shortly. "Nick and Ari from the tribes of the Jinn, come to visit and travel with our cousin Drake."

"Wouldn't it be safer just to stay hidden?"

"It's always better to hide in plain sight," Nico assured her, caressing her hand before letting go. "And I far prefer being your husband."

"But we're only pretending."

"For now." He agreed, but his eyes held a deeper message she was almost afraid to read.

"What do you know of the Jinn?" Nico tried to coach Riki—or Ari, as he should call her while they wore these roles—about the part she'd be playing. He'd be with her every step of the way, of course, but Nico believed in preparation for all contingencies.

"I know very little, I'm ashamed to admit. I think many of them make their living telling stories and playing music. Lucan had some of them entertain him every now and again until his...change became too great. I liked their songs."

"We are nomadic," Drake continued taking items from his satchel and placing them on the table as he spoke. "We go where life leads us and prefer to remain a mystery for the most part, which will serve your purpose well."

"We?" she asked, uncertainty on her face.

"I was adopted by one of the Jinn clans after performing a...service for the head family."

Nico was still amazed by some of the things Drake had gotten involved in during his time abroad. Few men could claim adoption by the secretive Jinn. Though Drake had never divulged the details of what he'd done to earn the rare honor, Nico had spent not a little time trying to puzzle it out. But this was one secret even the Spymaster of Draconia hadn't learned. Still, he knew Drake's contacts among the Jinn could be vital in their escape from this Mother-forsaken land.

Nico took the colorful silk scarf from Riki's hands and showed her the way Jinn women traditionally folded their headscarves. Luckily, he'd undressed his share of fiery Jinn wenches in his time and knew well how they assembled their clothing. This he taught to Riki, pleased when she proved to be a quick study.

He tied the scarf at a jaunty angle. The tendrils of fringe framed Riki's beautiful features. Her luminous eyes looked even bigger, if such a thing were possible, and Nico wanted nothing more than to take her back to bed and claim her fully as his own.

But he couldn't. Not yet. Not 'til she came to him freely. Nico was a patient man, but the dragon in him seethed, wanting its mate.

"We'll enter the tavern with Drake. He'll handle the performing."

"Won't the people expect all of us to perform?"

"Not me. I'll be wearing the marks of a warrior." Nico liked that she was asking questions. Overall, she seemed to be calmly absorbing everything they threw at her.

"The Jinn learn how to defend themselves and their women from a young age," Drake added. "No one will be surprised if Nick doesn't sing or dance. Not with his war face scaring everyone away from you, Ari."

The newly shortened version of her name made her start a bit, but not as much as it could have, Nico was pleased to see.

"As for you, *Ari*," Nico emphasized the new nickname to get her more used to it, "we'll claim you're too tired from the trip. Perhaps we can say you're pregnant. It would give us an excuse to retire early and explain your pale skin."

The more he thought about it, the more Nico liked the idea. Not just for their disguise, but for real. He'd love nothing more than to plant his child in Riki's womb, see her swell with it, and watch it being born. He'd never before wanted to be a father, but suddenly, it was one of the most important goals in his life. Soon, he promised himself, soon Riki would come to him and he would take her and they'd make babies together. Soon. The dragon side of his nature could barely wait.

But for now, Riki was blushing furiously at the idea of being pregnant, charming him, but worrying him at the same time. If she couldn't handle the role, people would become suspicious.

"We don't have to say that if it embarrasses you, sweetheart," he gave her the option.

"No. It's all right. If it'll help, I say let's do it. It sounds reasonable. It just took me by surprise."

"Right then, Ari, my love." He clasped her hands in his. "You're only just realizing you're pregnant. Just a few weeks into it, so you're still thin, but feeling the effects of morning sickness at all times of the day. If things get too rough for you in the common room, pretend to feel ill and I'll take you out, but it's important we make a short appearance at least, so no one will be surprised when we leave in Drake's wagon tomorrow morning."

"I won't let you down, Nico. I promise."

The common room of the tavern was raucous when they entered. Drake was greeted with a cheer and he held up his instrument of choice—a large-bodied lute—with a smile of triumph. Curious glances were sent their way as they entered behind the blond man, but Riki held her head high and smiled at the people who cheered for Drake.

Drake escorted them to his reserved table near the fire and turned to the crowd, quickly introducing his cousins from the Jinn and launching into a song before anyone could ask questions about them. He was good. He was actually damn good, Riki quickly realized. On par with, or better than, many of the famous bards who had entertained Lucan in the palace.

She recognized some of the tunes he played and found herself tapping her toes and humming along. Riki had always loved music of almost any kind and had hidden her enjoyment carefully from Lucan. He often had musicians play for him in his chambers, though it was more for effect than any true enjoyment, Riki secretly thought. Lucan was always too busy eating and plying his many lovers to bother listening to the music he demanded be played in the background. Only Riki truly enjoyed the music. One or two of the musicians had noted her interest, but were keen enough to keep their knowledge well hidden from the vindictive king.

Riki saw the pitying looks they gave her though, as they entered and left the chamber where she was kept chained. A few would smile at her kindly when nobody could see and some would play songs she particularly loved—sometimes she thought they played them just for her. Lucan could care less what ballad or dance tune was played, as long as there was music to accompany his pathetic seductions.

It was rather disgusting, really, but Riki never associated the music with the heinous acts she'd been forced to witness. No, the music had been her savior at such times, allowing her to focus on something with her ears, even while her eyes were forced to watch something abhorrent to her.

And Lucan made her watch. When, in the beginning, she'd tried to turn away, he'd had guards tie her and beat her until she complied with Lucan's desires. It seemed because he couldn't have her, he enjoyed taunting the virgin with his vile acts of sexual possession. Everything she knew about sexual perversions she'd learned from watching Lucan, but as long as there was music, she could focus on that, even while her eyes remained open and watching Lucan's disgusting tableaus.

The music was her salvation, her solace and her strength. No one knew just how deeply she loved it, though she thought one or two of the more sympathetic men who had been ordered to play for Lucan had begun to guess.

Drake launched into a sad ballad known as "Arundelle's Lament". It was a mythical tale about how the river bordering both Skithdron and Draconia in the north got its name. It told of the sad wizard woman, Arundelle, who lost her mate in the days when wizards still roamed the lands and magic was everywhere and in all things.

Riki loved Drake's version of the song and her eyes filled with tears at the particularly poignant verses. It was a long ballad with many stanzas and Riki sat entranced through each and every one, as did most of the room. Drake was truly gifted.

When the last note sounded, silence reigned through the crowded room. Seconds later, thunderous applause filled the air. Coppers and even a silver coin or two flew through the air to land in the pot at Drake's feet as he smiled and bowed to the cheering crowd. He picked up the pot of coins and sat it on the table between Riki and Nico as the applause died down.

"Thank you my friends," Drake addressed the crowd with a humble smile. "I must take a break now, but I'll play more for you after I've whet my whistle."

Groans and cajoling rose from the crowd, many trying to get Drake to play some more, but he politely declined, pulling out the big chair reserved for him. He drank heartily of the tankard a pretty lass placed before him. In fact, drinks were delivered for Riki and Nico too, simply because they were with Drake, so popular was he.

A burly man came over, wiping his hands on his apron and Riki realized this must be the landlord, or one of his family at least. Drake stood and shook the man's hand, introducing him to Nico and then briefly to Riki as Jonas Brewer. He seemed a pleasant sort of fellow with a kind smile, but Riki saw he had a shrewd eye for business and he ran his establishment with keen awareness of efficiency and potential for profit.

"Won't your cousins favor us with a song?" Brewer asked with a jovial smile. There was an undercurrent of urgency as well and Riki was instantly on alert for why the man seemed a bit anxious. Nico and Drake must have felt it as well, for both sat a little straighter in their chairs and Nico's gaze roved casually around the place, pausing only briefly by the door.

That was enough to make Riki look, and what she saw in her brief glance nearly gave her a heart attack. Four soldiers in uniform stood by the door surveying the crowd. Their uniforms signaled they weren't from the actual palace, so they wouldn't recognize her, but they were definitely looking for something. In fact, they were probably looking for *her*.

Riki remembered what Nico had said about hiding in plain sight and an idea formed in her mind. Gathering her courage, Riki looked over at Nico. His gaze was shifting casually around, noting exits and potential routes they might take, she realized, if things went badly. She had to do something to save herself. Nico had done everything to this point and she needed to take a more active role in her escape. It was fast becoming a matter of pride.

I can sing. Riki spoke those words privately to Nico alone, testing the waters before she jumped in.

Nico's gaze shot to hers, questioning.

You don't have to do anything. Let me take care of you, sweetheart.

That's all you've done is take care of me. I can do this, if it will help. If you need me to, I can sing, and rather well, so you won't be embarrassed. Though I'm nowhere near as good as Drake.

Are you sure?

Riki smiled at him as he reached across the table to take her hand in his. To anyone looking at them they seemed a young couple in love. Only they knew of the life or death situation they were in and the dire plans being hatched silently between them.

I can do it. If Drake will play for me.

Nico raised her hand to his lips and kissed her knuckles softly as his gaze moved subtly to the doorway. The soldiers were moving closer, she could see them out of the corner of her eye. It was time to act. Nico nodded slightly and turned to the landlord.

"My wife will sing a song for you while our cousin rests, if that is your wish."

Riki was impressed with the slight Jinn accent and foreign phrasing Nico used and her smile was genuine as she looked up at the landlord. Thankfully, Jinn women were seldom heard to speak to strangers, though they were rumored to be quite vocal among their own people.

"Are you sure, cousin Ari?" Drake asked with concern. "You don't have to if you feel ill." His hand shot out to take hers as she rose slowly from the table. The message in his blue eyes was clear. He worried for her, but she knew she could do this. It was about the only thing she could do to help herself—and these wonderful men who were protecting her.

"It's all right," she told him softly. Drake squeezed her hand once, then let go, reaching for his lute, but Nico's hand closed over the instrument's long neck first. Riki was surprised, but the dancing light in Nico's eyes warmed her.

"I will play for my lovely wife. We are still newlyweds, after all." Nico's laughter was echoed by Drake and the landlord, and soon the other tables around them were cheering as Riki and Nico faced the crowd.

The landlord faded back to the bar area. Riki could easily see the soldiers stopping, watching them speculatively for a moment before moving on. All she had to do now was sing convincingly enough and they would have no idea the prize they searched for was right under their noses.

"What song, my love?" Nico asked her softly.

Riki thought quickly of the many songs she'd committed to memory over the months she'd been subjected to Lucan's imprisonment. She needed something relatively short, that she could do well. After just a few seconds of deliberation, she thought of one the crowd would probably like as well.

"How about 'The Siren'?"

Nico looked surprised for a moment, and then smiled his devastatingly handsome smile. She was certain his smile alone charmed half the women in the room. Nico really was the most delectable rogue.

"Anything for you, my love." She heard several women sigh at the interplay while Nico stood at her side, one foot resting on a chair while he held the lute against his middle, propped on a raised knee. He began with a few introductory notes and Riki realized he had some skill with the instrument. Of course, he was a prince. He was probably schooled in all sorts of things most regular people never learned.

When he got to the part where she began to sing, a hush came over the room. Many recognized the popular tune apparently, and wanted to see how the young Jinn lass Riki was pretending to be would do with it. She opened her mouth, fear nearly overpowering her for one dark moment before she found that place within herself where the music lived. It was the place she had retreated to when Lucan had done his worst to hurt her, to ridicule her and break her. It was the place only music touched and it formed the basis of her soul.

Touching that vast power, she began to sing, knowing nothing could harm her while she was in that magical place.

Chapter Nine

Nico was uncertain of Riki's plan, but willing to give her this chance to prove herself. He knew, deep down, she had to do something to take control of her life, or live forever with fear. He'd seen it before with warriors he'd freed from long imprisonment. To a man, they needed to feel as if they were doing something in their own rescue or else live diminished for the rest of their lives.

There were only four soldiers in the tavern. Chances were, if they became overly suspicious, Nico and Drake could handle them, so it was with well calculated risk he allowed Riki to take the stage and sing.

But when her mouth opened and the song came pouring out, Nico was nearly as entranced as the patrons of the tavern. Her voice was magical, enthralling and pure. She had the attention of every person in the room within the first few notes of the haunting song, and kept it throughout.

The song spoke of a sea siren who cried for the men she unwillingly killed as they sought her out in the depths of her ocean home. The melody was especially haunting and the words touching. Nico had always liked the song, but he'd never heard it better performed than in that moment. Riki was powerful indeed, though her power came not in any physical way, but rather in her ability to bedevil and beguile with just her voice.

Every man in the tavern was watching her, hanging on every note from her luscious lips, wanting her. A possessive pride rose up in Nico's dragon soul. This was *his* mate! *His* woman that had such gifts. Others could watch her, but they'd never have her. They'd never hold her the way he would. This he vowed as the dragon within preened with pride and a bit of awe at the phenomenal woman the Mother of All had seen fit to mate with him.

The song had only a few stanzas and a haunting chorus. It was over soon enough and as with Drake's longer performance, silence greeted the last note, followed by thunderous applause as the last chord faded away. Coins rained down on them both, landing in the emptied pot Drake hastily put at their feet. Riki curtsied shyly, her pale face becomingly rosy while Nico handed Drake back his lute with finality. They'd done their song to convince the soldiers they were truly Jinn entertainers. He would not subject Riki to more, no matter how much the crowd begged.

Drake accepted the lute with a flourish and a wink as he replaced them in the center of the room and broke into a happy, complicated tune on his lute. Soon the crowd was clapping along, stomping their feet, and a few were even dancing on the edges of the crowd. Nico noted the departure of the soldiers and acted the part of the crafty Jinn, emptying their winnings from the pot into his pocket and replacing the empty pot at Drake's feet for the next round.

He kept Riki next to him, one arm possessively around her shoulders as people sent drinks and sweets to them, in thanks for her song. She was definitely popular with the crowd, but what surprised Nico most was the women liked her just as well as the men. She had touched a chord with them, her voice reaching through to all in the room, not inspiring lust, but instead, ringing with the beauty of the words of the song, creating looks of wonder on all their faces.

There was something more to Riki's voice. Nico could feel it. But he wasn't quite sure what it was, only that it was somehow magical. This would bear further study and thought, when they had time to explore what her voice could truly do.

It sounded far-fetched, even to him, but then, Riki's twin could shift to dragon form. Who said Riki hadn't found some other way to channel the immense dragon magic within her soul?

"Would you and your lady favor us with another song?" The jovial landlord was back at their table, but Nico turned the man down with a regretful sigh.

"I fear not, good sir. My wife is newly with child and tires easily these early days."

The man smiled broadly, offering his congratulations as Riki snuggled closer to Nico, feigning fatigue very well indeed. She was a natural at this sort of thing and he couldn't be prouder of her. There could be no more perfect mate for the Prince of Spies.

"Well, if I can't convince you, the room next to your cousin's is all ready for you. Drake arranged it this morning when he got word of your arrival." The landlord took up two empty tankards in one big hand and swiped the table dry with a cloth he kept at his waist. "I know you'll be taking your leave early in the morn, so I'll wish you well now and hope you'll return to visit us the next time you're in the city."

Nico shook the man's free hand, surprised only a little by the secret gesture he made with his thumb. No wonder Drake stayed here when he was in Plinth. This man was part of the Brotherhood of the Jinn. Nico gave him the return sign and a wide grin split the man's face as he nodded once and bustled off. Nico realized they had friends in Plinth he hadn't even known about. Aligning with the Jinn—something Drake had managed to accomplish long ago, and Nico more recently—was turning out to be a very good thing, indeed.

Riki was content to let Nico handle arrangements and guide her actions. Once the soldiers left the tavern, the real fatigue of the escape, the journey, her residual weakness from the beatings and starvation and the let-down from the terrifying fear that those soldiers would raise the alarm all collided within her. Riki was drained and weak, more than happy to lean on Nico and let him lead the way down the dim hall to their room.

They went into the room just before Drake's, and Riki let Nico settle her on the side of a large bed, offering no protest when he removed the scarf from her hair, then the jewelry. He left the ring on her finger, and kept his own on as well, which touched her for some odd reason. They weren't mated in the tradition of the Jinn, but they wore the symbols, and it pleased some inner desire she hadn't even recognized.

When he tugged at her dress, she protested. Sitting at her side on the edge of the large bed, Nico grasped her hands in his.

"I won't hurt you, Riki. I promise."

"I know you won't," she replied softly, "but I can't give you my virginity. It's my only protection from Lucan and his men. Please understand."

Nico's lips thinned, but he seemed to swallow whatever argument he wanted to make. Instead, he pulled her into his arms, holding her close to his heart.

"I do understand, but know this, Arikia. A time will come when you will give yourself to me willingly." His words were strong and sure, sending bolts of excitement through her warm body. "I will never force you, never take you without your consent, never seduce you into anything. You will come to me willingly, or not at all. Is that clear?"

She nodded against his chest. "Yes, Nico. Thank you." The relief was heartfelt. Riki knew Nico was a man of his word. If he said she would be given the choice of her own free will, then she believed him.

"Do you trust me?"

"I do," she said softly, knowing the truth of those words in her heart.

"Then lie with me tonight. Skin to skin. I promise I will not take your virginity this night or tomorrow morn, but I need to feel you against me, sweetheart, like I need my next breath."

And she could feel the need trembling through his strong muscles, so close under her cheek beneath his shirt. If she truly trusted him—and she did—she would do as he requested, but there was one problem.

She didn't trust herself.

Still, she wanted to feel Nico's skin against hers. The idea was too tantalizing to resist and she had his promise of safety as long as she didn't willingly request his lovemaking. Moving back, Riki allowed him to remove her colorful dress, leaving her bare before him.

Silently, Nico tucked her into the big bed, care in his every move. He moved away then, to secure his belongings and turn down the lamp for the night, leaving the room bathed in a soft golden glow. He returned to the bedside, catching her eye before stripping out of his clothes right in front of her. It was as if he wanted her to see each and every inch of his glorious body as it was revealed.

He was lean and hard muscled, bulging where it counted most. His arms were thick and strong, as were the muscles of his thighs and calves. His belly was ridged with muscle like a washboard and his chest was a thing of beauty. Nico held her gaze, daring her to look at that part of him that most wanted to claim her, and slowly, she dropped her gaze.

He was rampant, hard and wanting, his cock long and thick. Riki wondered how in the world such a glorious thing could fit inside her untried body, and she found herself wanting to find out.

But that would never do. She had to resist such thoughts, even with male perfection standing right in front of her. Her chastity was the only thing protecting her. Give that up and she gave up her life as well.

Still, Riki found herself growing warm, her blood firing and swirling in her veins. Had the mere sight of a naked man ever caused this kind of reaction in her before? She knew it had not. She'd seen Lucan and his lovers of both sexes. The men were fit and trim with good bodies—Lucan demanded only the best—but none had evoked this heated response. No other man had ever affected her like Nico and she knew in her heart, no other man ever would.

"You're so beautiful, my Riki." Nico whispered as he knelt on the side of the bed.

He had it all wrong, she thought. Nico was the beautiful one. Apprehension filled her as he levered himself down on the bed and folded the covers back, exposing her bare body to his hungry gaze.

"I want you so badly. I'm a desperate man, sweetheart." Nico chuckled at himself. "But I already care far too much to rush you." He smoothed one large hand down from her neck, over the rise of her breasts, pausing to tease one hard nipple and then lower, tracing the curve of her waist. "I need you like I need my next breath. Give me this," he whispered, his lips against her mouth, "just this, so I can go on living."

Nico kissed her then, his tongue probing gently at her lips, parting them and sweeping inside. Riki shivered, the feel of his tongue, the warm cinnamon taste of him firing her senses as his hard body covered hers, his arms imprisoning her in welcome warmth and spiraling tendrils of desire. His tongue played with hers, daring her to follow where he would lead.

There was a playfulness to Nico's lovemaking. A fresh sense of wonder filled her. This man made her feel cherished. It was a secure feeling, one that begged her to give everything she had in return.

But she couldn't. Her very life was at stake. She'd be a fool to trade her life for a moment's pleasure. Even with Nico.

He moved then, pulling back to look down into her eyes as his hands moved on her body. One hand cupped her breast, massaging gently as her desire peaked. His other roving hand found her core. Nico held her gaze as he slid a finger inside her channel, teasing, testing, tantalizing her almost beyond reason. His thumb played over her clit, making her squirm as passion threatened to overwhelm her.

Then he lowered his head. Nico's warm breath feathered over her nipple a moment before his mouth closed over the taut peak. A moan bubbled up from her throat as pleasure radiated from her nipple to her womb. At the same time, his fingers were sending shockwaves of sensation from her clit and that dastardly finger started pulsing in and out of her tight channel.

Riki couldn't take much more.

"Come for me, sweetheart." Nico's whispered words encouraged her as she came with a little cry, captured by his lips against hers.

The pleasure peaked higher than before, lasting long, long moments as he continued to pet her damp body. She was wrung out utterly when at last the sensations died down. Nico kissed her long and with a tenderness that brought tears to her eyes.

"Sleep now, sweet Riki. We have a long day ahead of us."

"But what about you?"

He kissed her forehead as he moved back. "This was for you, sweetheart. To show you how much I care. To prove you could trust me."

"But I do trust you." She protested lightly when he spooned her from behind, his hard cock settling into the crack of her ass as if it belonged there. "I don't want you to suffer for my pleasure."

Nico chuckled, low and sexy in her ear. "Does it feel like I'm suffering?"

She had no answer to that as he pumped his cock through the warm crevice of her butt cheeks. He purred in her ear, surprising her as passion stirred a bit within her.

"Go to sleep, Riki. I'll be fine."

"But—"

"Sleep." He cut off her protests with a gentle squeeze of her waist, his hand moving to cup her breast and pull gently on the nipple. "That's an order."

She felt him settle behind her, but Riki's restless mind kept her awake. Nico was such a special man. She doubted any other man would have put her pleasure above his own. Nico was a prince—both literally and figuratively. She had to smile at the thought as she snuggled back against him. He was asleep, but even in sleep, he cradled her body gently, his still semi-hard cock nestling against her.

Riki wished she dared take him fully, but she was so desperately afraid. She wanted him, of that there was no doubt, but she feared what would happen after she gave herself to him.

Would he desert her? She thought not, but she really had no way of knowing for sure. Even more importantly, would they be recaptured by Lucan? If so, her purity was the only thing saving her. Could she give up her one protection?

Riki just wasn't sure. In fact, she wasn't sure about anything. Her heart was in turmoil. Strange new feelings were churning within her for this special man who held her so close in the night, with little thought for his own comfort. It would be so easy to fall in love with Nico. Riki was afraid she was half in love with him already. But did he—could he—love her in return?

Nico was a prince, and no matter what he claimed about her heritage, she was just a runaway slave. From the moment she'd been stolen from her home and family, she'd been a possession, a plaything, a pawn to be traded and bartered among men more powerful than she. Riki would never go back to that, but she knew all too well, she might not have any choice in the matter. If she were captured, all her options would be gone.

It really all boiled down to this moment, and this man. Riki turned in his arms, looking her fill at his handsome face, relaxed now in sleep. He really was beautiful, both inside and out. And he was caring and selfless as well. She'd learned that firsthand.

Nico had been so kind to her, so gentle. Oh, how she wished she could make love to him fully. She knew he would be a generous, kind and caring lover. The longing for his cock welled within her, dampening her pussy and making her squirm.

She dared not take him where she wanted him most, but she'd already sampled his cum and wanted more. Looking down between their bodies, she saw he was still semi-erect. It would take little, she guessed, to bring him back to full hardness and then to the same height of pleasure he'd given her.

Gathering her courage, Riki worked her way down his body with her mouth and hands, placing little kisses here and there, licking and lapping at his hard ridges and the flat nipples, making her way to the ultimate goal.

Nico's eyes shot open as he felt a soft tongue swirling around his nipple.

Riki.

He spied just the top of her head, working downward on his body as Riki kissed and licked him awake in the most delightful way. The little princess was an adventuress.

"I hope you know what you're getting into."

His voice seemed to startle her. Riki stopped, her soft hands around his cock, and looked up at him. Nico nearly groaned at the glazed passion he read in her lovely green eyes. The light was dim, but his vision was keener than most humans. Being half dragon had its advantages, after all.

"You don't mind, do you?" Her sultry voice teased his senses.

"Mind?" His breath hitched as she moved back down, her hands tightening on his hard cock a moment before she reached down with her tongue to lick the tip. Nico stifled a groan. "I don't mind at all."

He reached back and grabbed on to the rails in the headboard—anything to keep from grabbing her and pinning her under his body while he took what she refused to give. He wanted to fuck her desperately, but he'd made a vow. She would come to him willingly or not at all.

Riki smiled up at him before returning her full concentration to the matter at hand. She took his cock in one dainty hand, guiding it into her hot, wet mouth, while the fingers of her other devilish little hand massaged his balls. Fire shot from his groin, pleasure filling his senses as she found the spot just behind his heavy sac that brought him even higher.

"Riki, love, you're killing me."

Riki took him all the way down until the tip of his cock nudged the back of her throat. Then she sucked, strong and long, and he nearly lost it. Nico tangled his hands in her hair, trying to raise her up, but she only followed his lead so far. No, this little vixen knew what she wanted and she wanted it now.

Who was he to deny her?

Nico lay back, leaving one of his hands in her hair simply because he liked the feel of the soft strands under his fingers. Riki moved on him, increasing her tempo as she massaged his balls, positioning herself between his legs on her knees for better leverage. Then the little witch moved one of her clever hands downward, massaging his ass. Nico thought he would die when one of her wet fingers found the tight hole there and pushed within.

Riki set up a gentle, driving rhythm with her mouth on his cock, one hand squeezing his balls and one finger delving within his ass, massaging from the inside. Nico knew he was lost.

He groaned deep as he came in her mouth. Riki swallowed every drop, catching the overflow on her tongue and licking him down deep with every spasm of his pleasure-wracked body. Never had he come so hard in a woman's mouth.

Nico knew in that moment she'd well and truly ruined him for any other woman. And he didn't mind in the least. It was

Riki or no one, from this moment forward. She was his and he was most definitely hers, in every possible way.

Nico panted, trying to catch his breath as he came down from the highest peak he'd ever reached with just oral stimulation. Riki purred contentedly at his side, stroking his body even as she snuggled into his form, tired and sated almost as if she'd needed his cum to make her complete—to allow her to relax and sleep.

The thought warmed him as he held her close.

"Thank you, my darling Riki," he whispered, bending to kiss her sweet, puffy lips. When he pulled back, she blinked up at him, sleepy, with lazy, passion-glazed eyes.

"It was my pleasure." Her smile told him that indeed, she had found pleasure in pleasing him and Nico counted himself among the luckiest men in the world in that moment. His mate cared for his comfort. She was choosing him, whether she realized it or not. This was one big step closer to his goal. She would be his! Sooner rather than later, if this was any indication.

"Sleep now, sweetheart." He turned her in his arms and she was asleep before he settled. Her trust in him was that complete.

Nico fell asleep once more—deeper this time—replete with the knowledge his mate was coming to trust him, maybe even love him as much as he already loved her.

They set out at first light in Drake's shiny blue wagon. He had a team of gorgeous, matched white horses to pull the wagon, which was closed in on the sides and back, with a locking door at either end. Inside, Riki found a sumptuous living space with a giant, down-stuffed mattress and a multitude of soft pillows in bright hues.

Drake's clothes took up one cupboard, while musical instruments were packed carefully all around. Food and cooking items were in another few cupboards and extra blankets and furs filled another. All in all, Drake seemed well-stocked for any contingency. This was truly a home on wheels and Riki had never seen the like.

The men rode up front on the plank seat, leaving Riki to the inside of the wagon, both to hide her as they rode out of the city, and because Jinn women were usually well-hidden in the light of day. The men dealt with the outside world while the women ruled the roost, or so the sayings went. Jinn women were usually only seen in a professional capacity, as singers, musicians, dancers, fortune tellers, and the like, and then always watched carefully by their warrior males. Jinn men were very protective of their women, which worked to their advantage in trying to get Riki out of the city without raising any suspicion.

They left the city gates behind with little fanfare. A few of the guards asked Drake when he thought he might be back, indicating they enjoyed his music and would welcome a return visit. The usual stuff, she supposed, as she listened from within the safety of the wagon, holding her breath to see if they would be stopped and searched.

But luck was with them and they left the city behind easily enough. It was almost anti-climactic after what they'd been through to get this far, but Riki thanked the fates that allowed her to get even this distance from Lucan. Every step of the horses took her farther away from his madness and closer to freedom.

After an hour or two, Nico knocked on the little door at the front of the wagon, directly behind the plank seat. Scrambling to open it, Riki peeped out, curious about their location.

“Are you all right in there?” Nico asked quietly, his eyes searching hers.

She nodded. “It’s very comfortable.”

“You could leave this door open now, if you want some fresh air. We haven’t passed anyone on this road in a while. Chances are the traffic will be light from here on out. Not much comes down from the north this time of year.”

“Where are we going?” Riki asked, smiling as she secured the door back so it wouldn’t swing shut with the swaying movement of the wagon.

“North to the Jinnfaire,” Drake answered. “It’s a gathering of the Jinn near the northern border of Skithdron. This time at least. It’s in a different place each time.” Drake shrugged. “Word came down a few weeks ago that the Jinnfaire was being called and where. It works to our advantage right now, so that’s where we’re going.”

“Do they gather often?” Riki fought her fatigue as the wagon swayed.

“No, not at all. This is the first Jinnfaire called in more than a decade.” Drake smiled at her then turned his attention back to the team of horses.

“Why don’t you get some rest, sweetheart?” Nico caught her yawning and motioned her back into the wagon. “We’ve got quite a ways to go and you’re still recovering.”

“There’s lots of food back there too,” Drake piped in. “Feel free to eat anything you like. We can get more and I usually carry provisions for several months. It will only take a day or so to get to the Jinnfaire.”

Riki yawned again. “I think I’ll do that. Wake me if you need me, all right?”

The men agreed and she sank back into the shadowed interior of the wagon, heading straight for the fluffy, inviting bed.

Chapter Ten

Riki collapsed into exhausted sleep in the back of the wagon while Nico and Drake rode up front. She was safe back there, Nico knew, well hidden from anyone who might pass.

"She's got the magic, you know. I recognized it the moment she started singing last night." Drake's voice was contemplative as he drove the wagon in the silent morn.

"There's something...but I don't know what it is exactly," Nico finally admitted.

"It's the Jinn magic. Some of them have it, but I've never felt it as strongly as last night. She can influence people with her song. It's a secret among the Jinn, known only to the bards among them."

"Which is most of them," Nico put in as Drake nodded in agreement.

"True, but it *is* still a secret. Did you never wonder why Jinn musicians are so sought after? It's their ability to sway a crowd or even a single listener in whatever way they wish. Last night, your girl had every last person in that common room under her spell, to do with what she willed. It's a dangerous and amazing gift."

"She's not even aware of it, I don't think."

"Then it's even more dangerous. We need to get her to the Jinnfaire for more than just her physical safety. I can teach her a little, but I don't have a strong gift—not like the real Jinn. They'll be able to teach her how to control it and use it. Most especially, how to use it safely."

Riki surprised the men by sleeping through the entire day. Nico checked on her a few times, pausing to brush her lovely hair back from her face. The poor waif was just exhausted. Lucan had kept her starved, beaten and without much sleep for far too long. Her body was catching up, eating well for the first time in years, not having to deal with new bruises every few days, and sleeping her fill.

Nico lingered, watching her breathe. He'd fallen for this small woman so deeply, so instantly, even he was a little surprised by the intensity of his feelings. Still, he knew how it was for dragons and knights. They invariably knew almost from the moment they met their destined mate and dropped hard and fast into love that lasted a lifetime. Nico hadn't thought he'd ever find the woman who could do that to him, but he was happy to find he'd been so gloriously wrong.

True, he'd been a little envious of his older brother, Roland, when he'd first seen how happy Roland was with Lana. But Lana hadn't had the effect on Nico that Riki did. No matter that they were twins, it was Riki's bright soul that made him love her.

"She still sleeping?" Drake asked with sympathy as Nico climbed back onto the plank seat from the back of the wagon. He let the curtain drop in front of the little door so the fading sunlight wouldn't bother Riki as she slept.

"She needs the rest." Nico nodded as he got as comfortable as he could on the padded seat.

"I heard rumors from other Jinn about her, though I didn't know who she was at the time. The Jinn have been keeping an eye on her, holding her in their prayers. She'll be welcome among them for what she suffered, if nothing else."

"That's a hell of a reason to be welcome." Nico sighed heavily.

"What's most important now is that she's safe with you. We'll get her across the border with the help of the Jinn."

"Will we?" Nico let the despair of their situation nearly overwhelm him for a moment. He tried so hard to keep a positive attitude—especially in front of Riki—but every once in a while he had his doubts about how he'd keep her safe during their attempt to cross the border.

"We will." Drake faced him, his eyes hard. "Of that, have no doubt."

"I hope your Jinn brethren will be as sure, and as helpful as you believe."

"If worse comes to worst, Nico, I'll stand for you. My word has some pull with the Jinn. At the very least, they'll have to let us leave unmolested if they become hostile. They have rules among the Brotherhood and well I know them."

Nico clapped his old friend on the back. "I'm glad you're here, Drake. I couldn't ask for better help on this journey, and I'm not too proud to admit my lady and I may need every bit of your skill and aid before this is all over."

"It's what I'm here for," Drake smiled. "I serve the kingdom—and you, Nicolas. When I swore myself to your service, it was for life, and it was not done lightly."

Nico nodded, touched by Drake's heartfelt words. "It was not taken lightly on my part either, Drake. Your home is in Draconia and it will always be."

"But my role is best played in other lands. At least for now." A shadow of old pain crossed Drake's chiseled face and Nico knew he was thinking of his family and the harsh words that had passed between father and son before he left home on his chosen path.

Though in truth, two fathers had raised him, it was clear from the shining blond hair and roguish features, which of the knights was his sire. Sir Declan was a hard man, with few words of kindness for the son that was so much like him. But Declan was an exemplary knight, aide to the king himself, and greatly respected. It had been hard for Drake, at the young age of fifteen, to live up to his example—and his expectations.

"Your family loves you, no matter what path you choose."

Nico saw the grimace on Drake's face but the other man spoke no more on the subject. Some wounds were too painful to probe. Nico understood that.

"We'd best make camp before it gets too dark," Drake said quietly some moments later. "I know a relatively safe place just ahead."

The site Drake promised was as good as any and better than most in this land of skiths and hostile soldiers. Bordered on three sides by high rocks that would make it impossible for man or skith to approach, only one flank needed to be guarded and that could be accomplished easily enough by laying fires in the stone pits already in place for just such purpose.

"This is a regular stopping place for the Jinn who travel this road. I'm a little surprised we're the only ones here, but with the Jinnfaire so close, I suppose they've all moved on farther north." Drake was busy, dragging wood from the fringes of the trees and supplementing it with some of the supply he kept stored under his wagon. Fire was a necessity if you wanted to spend the night camping in Skithdron unmolested.

When he would have set to work sparking flame off rock and blade, Nico nudged him aside. Calling up just a touch of his dragon heat, he set the kindling to smoldering and within moments a cheery blaze was going.

"Nice." Drake chuckled as they repeated the process in the other two fire pits, set in a line in front of the wagon that was now snuggly protected on all sides—from skiths at least.

"I'd better wake Riki. She'll want to wash up and she should eat." Nico headed for the wagon, entering soundlessly so as not to startle his sleeping princess.

A gentle nibble on her cheek first woke Riki. Her hand rose to brush away the distraction, but it was captured in a warm hand and her palm placed over a stubbly cheek.

Nico.

His name ran through her mind as his lips claimed hers in a joyous, gentle, loving kiss. Riki stretched under him, enjoying the way his hands molded her waist and brushed along her thighs as his lips played with hers.

At length he pulled back.

"Good evening, sweetheart."

"What time is it?" Riki wanted to look out the door of the little wagon, but her eyes stayed glued to Nico. He was so handsome and so kind.

"It's just before sunset and we're setting up camp for the night."

"I'm all turned around. Staying up all night and sleeping all day. I don't know what time it is at all."

Nico chuckled and kissed her forehead before moving back. "It's all right. You can wash up in the nearby stream, then we'll all have a nice dinner and settle in for the evening. It's too risky to keep traveling by wagon at night with the possibility of skith attack."

That woke Riki fully to the continued danger. She sat up and stretched, leaving the wagon moments later. Nico kept watch for her while she washed up at the stream, then it was back to the campsite to see if she could help with dinner preparations, but the men had things well in hand.

Drake had things set up along the bottom and sides of his wagon so everything he needed was within easy reach. Riki marveled at the hidden compartments built into the blue wagon. Some of them were truly ingenious and she was certain he wasn't showing her everything. He was a spy, after all.

Dinner was delicious and more so because of the company. Nico was attentive, filling her plate and refilling her cup when it ran empty, and the conversation was friendly and amusing. Drake told stories of his travels and some of the escapades he and Nico had gotten up to as youngsters. Riki understood better the deep bonds between the two men and she envied their tales of a carefree childhood and close friendship.

Nico was so perfect, so caring. She blessed the day he'd come to her and taken her out of her misery with Lucan. Nico was magical—a dragon of legend—and a man that made her heart beat faster with undeniable attraction.

So much had happened in so short a time, it was difficult for Riki to take it all in. Nico had swooped in at the least likely moment and rescued her from a sadistic tyrant, flying her away with him and keeping her safe. Add to that the incredible attraction she felt for him—even before she knew he could possibly free her—and Nico was a potent temptation she longed for with all her heart.

Why was she so zealously guarding her purity anyway? Now, fully rested and thinking more clearly as Drake strummed a quiet tune on his lute and they sat around the fire savoring a delicious port wine, Riki thought over her options. While it was true her virginity had protected her from the worst of Lucan's perversions, Riki knew his temper. She also knew by escaping as she had, should Lucan ever manage to recapture her, he would not go easy. He would beat and torture her in every way he could, as punishment for defying him. He'd done it before.

Lucan was so crazed at this point, she wasn't sure he wouldn't kill her. The reasoning part of his brain had seemed to be in less and less control of late, as the evil animal inside him took over. Lucan could easily kill her and she knew it would not likely be a quick or easy death. No, Lucan would make her pay cruelly before finally ending her life.

So what did it matter if she was virgin or not? In one way, he might kill her quicker if she lost her healing power. Once Lucan discovered she was no longer of use to him in that way, his rage might cause him to strike her down quickly. She could only pray for such an end if he did manage to recapture her.

Or she could kill herself before Lucan had the chance to do so. Riki wondered if she had the courage to do it if capture became inevitable. She wasn't sure, but if it came down to death at her own hands versus slow, painful, torturous death at Lucan's, she thought she just might choose the former. The lovely, sharp blade Drake had bought and Nico had given her ought to do the trick. She wore it now, as they told her most Jinn women did, tied discreetly to her thigh under her skirts. There was even a small slit in her pocket through which to access it without raising her skirt. Jinn women were apparently skilful in their own defense and Riki thought it must be nice to be Jinn—to be free to roam wherever the wind took you and live your life on your own terms.

A copper coin landed in her lap and Riki turned from her ruminations to look over at Nico. His smile was warm and engaging. He nodded toward the copper penny.

"For your thoughts," he said, tempting her to tease him right back.

"Oh, they're worth more than this, I'm sure."

Nico chuckled and dug into his pocket, leaning over and showering a handful of coins into her lap.

"This is just part of what you earned with your beautiful song last night." He shrugged. "It's yours anyway, but I'm still curious about what put such a hard expression on your face."

But Riki didn't want to revisit the dark thoughts. Instead, she played with the tinkling coins, running them through her fingers. She'd never had any coins of her own. Not like this.

"I really did earn these, didn't I?" The thought astounded her.

Drake ended his song on the lute. "You could make quite a living as a bard, milady. When you're tired of Nick here, why don't you look me up? We could make beautiful music together."

His comic leer made her laugh, though Nico bristled a bit in good-natured fun. These men were both so special to her. The Mother of All had been smiling on her when She put Riki into Nico's path.

"I'm sorry, Drake. My heart belongs to Nico."

The thought slipped out before she could censor her words. She heard Nico gasp and she dared to peer over at him in the firelight. He looked stunned. A little like she felt.

Did she love him?

Did she dare?

The answer came back in a heartbeat...a resounding yes. Riki's heart sped as she realized the truth. She was in love—deeply in love—with Nico. There was no denying it. No going back now.

She loved him.

Riki never thought she'd ever feel anything like this light, buoyant feeling. She never thought she'd have the chance. But the knowledge that she loved Nico sang through her soul, lighting the dark places and bringing hope where only moments before there was despair.

The feeling shocked her down to her toes and she wanted a chance to hug it tight, to bask in it and examine it, but Nico was looking at her strangely. He eyed her as if he knew something was going on in her mind and it had to do with him.

Guzzling the last of her port, Riki stood somewhat awkwardly from her seat by the fire.

"I'm going in. Goodnight, Drake. Nico." They'd discussed earlier how she would sleep in the back of the wagon while the men would take turns on watch and sleeping in the front.

Riki knew she was being a coward, but she had to think this through. She had to reevaluate her decisions in light of this new discovery. Love changed everything. At least it did for her. She'd never been in love before, and it changed all her perceptions of what was most important.

Nico.

Nico was the most important thing in her life. Not her safety. Not her worries about being recaptured by Lucan's men. Not anything else but Nico and making him happy.

And she knew just how to do it, but she was still afraid.

Only the fear had shifted from the possible consequences of making love with Nico to the actual act itself. She was a virgin and though she'd seen Lucan take his lovers in every which way, she'd never experienced it herself. She was afraid it would hurt. And she feared looking like a fool.

Though she knew Nico would be patient and kind, she still didn't want to disappoint him with her lack of experience. She'd quickly given up on the idea of remaining virgin. That seemed so insignificant now, when faced with the possibility of never making love to the man she loved. No, she wanted Nico more than anything—her own safety, her healing powers—anything.

"Riki?" Nico came to her inside the wagon, concern on his handsome features and she knew she was lost. "What's wrong?" He took her in his arms as she trembled, her decision made.

"Make love to me, Nico," she whispered in his ear, nibbling softly on his earlobe. "I don't want to be a witch anymore. I want you to make love to me."

Nico pulled back, shock clear on his face. Shock and a tender blooming passion in his eyes.

"You'd give up your only protection from Lucan for me?"

"I'd rather die than not be with you."

The breath caught in Nico's chest. He felt it too. He needed her so badly, he would give up anything—his home, his title, his family, even his life—just to be with her. Nico wanted her with a passion unsurpassed by anything else in his life. She was his. It was just that simple.

"I want you so desperately, my Arikia."

His stark words seemed to stun her as her eyes filled with tears. But they were tears of joy, Nico knew, because he was feeling the same wonder as their souls reached out to each other, forming tentative bonds that would only grow stronger with time.

"Oh, Nico!" Riki reached up to kiss him so deeply, so tenderly, it touched his very soul. When she pulled back, tears were streaming down her face. "I need you too. So much. I never thought..."

Nico crushed her to his chest, reveling in the moment. Never before had he wanted so desperately to hear those words from a woman. In fact, he'd never said them before to any woman of his acquaintance. Until this moment—this woman—he had never truly loved before. It was all perfectly clear. Riki was his destiny, as he was hers. Together they would face the rest of their lives, however long or short that may be.

How he wanted her! And he would have her, but she had to know the truth first.

"Riki, my darling, I'm honored you would willingly give up your power and your only protection, for me. You'll never know how much that gift means to me." He stroked back her hair tenderly. "But you need to know, you won't lose anything except your maidenhead when I take you. Your gifts will remain and will only grow stronger with time."

She blinked up at him skeptically.

"Are you certain? Lucan always said—"

"I don't know where that maniac got the idea, but it's totally false. Your sisters and mother are married and certainly not virgins, and their powers are among the strongest in the land. You won't lose your gifts, believe me." He kissed her forehead, unable to resist nibbling on her soft cheeks.

"But Loralie the witch told him it was so."

Nico straightened, but didn't release her. He would never let her out of his arms again, if he had his way.

"Loralie seems to be involved in much where the safety of Draconia is concerned, but whether for good or ill, ultimately, I cannot clearly say."

"When Lucan allied with King Salomar, part of the bargain was that Loralie would come to Lucan and treat him...turn him into what you saw."

"Try to merge him with the skiths? Is that what they were doing?"

Riki trembled in his arms as she nodded.

"And Loralie told Lucan you'd lose your healing gift if not a virgin." Nico rubbed comforting circles on her back as he held her, thinking through all the information he had on Lucan's sinister doings. "It might surprise you to know that Loralie also told your sister you'd be found in Skithdron."

"Why would she do that?" Riki's spine stiffened as she regained some of her composure.

"I begin to suspect she's not quite as evil—at least not in some of her actions—as we have always believed. Perhaps she told Lucan to keep you virgin to spare you rape and sexual torture by that evil creature she'd helped create."

"I don't understand why she would help me even that much."

Nico rubbed her shoulders, needing to refocus her mind on much more pleasant matters. "It will all come clear in time, I'm sure. But for now, sweetheart, I believe we have more important matters to tend to."

"Such as?" She smiled up at him coquettishly, making his heart stutter a bit at her beauty. She never failed to steal his breath.

"Pleasure, my sweet virgin. For us both. But especially for you. This first time, I want you to learn the pleasure I can bring you. I want you to enjoy every moment. If anything I do bothers you, I expect you to tell me right away."

Riki looked up into his eyes, smiling her trust in him. It was a heady responsibility and one he would cherish for the rest of their lives. Gently, he lowered his head, touching his lips to hers in a brief salute as he drew her closer against his straining erection.

She tasted of honey and roses, sweet and pure. Nico feared she was too good for the likes of him, but he didn't have the strength to let her go. No, he wanted her all to himself for the rest of their lives. Nico had finally found his mate and he would cherish her and hold her close forevermore.

But first he would claim her.

Nico coaxed her tongue into his mouth, sucking lightly, enjoying her little whimpers of excitement. She was so new to this kind of loveplay she squeaked and Nico relished his role as teacher. He'd never had a virgin before and he knew with certainty, he would never have another woman ever again. Only Riki.

It might take some time to talk her around to believing that, but he'd enjoy every moment of it. Still, Nico decided to go as slow as he could so as not to scare her off. Riki was still a little skittish, with good reason, and he wouldn't risk losing her because he'd pushed too far, too fast.

"Nico," she moaned into his mouth and the sound had him straining against her.

As gently as he could manage, he tugged her pretty dress up over her shoulders, parting from her only enough to remove the barrier between them. Her fingers went to the ties of his shirt, inflaming him. She was eager and ready, nearly desperate for what he could give her and Nico's chest pounded with satisfaction and desperate hunger.

"Do you know how special you are?" he whispered against her ear as he moved downward, his mouth worshiping her skin.

"Can you feel what you do to me?" Nico ground his hips forward into her thighs, relishing her softness against his very hard cock. "You set me on fire, Arikia. Only you."

He trailed his lips down her soft body, pausing along the way to tease her breasts, but also stopping here and there to kiss the scars left behind by her ordeal as Lucan's prisoner. Nico knew she needed his tenderness as well as his passion. She'd undoubtedly seen things that would make her afraid of what could occur between a man and woman. In light of that, Riki's willingness to make love with him astounded and humbled him.

Pausing to lick a small scar that traced down her abdomen to her belly button, he delved inside the little indentation with his tongue. Riki's girlish giggle as he tickled her was music to Nico's ears. That's what he wanted. He wanted to release her carefree nature, to reach the woman who should have been sheltered and loved all her life and never known a moment's pain. Nico knew he couldn't take away all the hardships she'd faced, but he could shower her with love and caring for the rest of her days. And he would.

But first he would make her his in every possible way.

Nico's mouth trailed down her body until he came to rest, kneeling before her. Looking upward, Nico met and held her shocked gaze as he lifted one of her sweet thighs over his shoulder. Nico smiled with satisfaction as the dragon in him trumpeted. This woman was his!

Leaning forward, he licked the little button of her clit, loving the gasping moan that issued from her lips and the warm cream that slid from her opening. With gentle fingers, he played at her entrance, coating his hands with her cream, sliding first one, then two fingers within, stretching her just a bit for what was to come.

Riki couldn't believe what Nico was doing. He had her spread wickedly over his shoulder, held mostly immobile to his desires. And she loved every minute of it—every lick, every touch, every teasing motion of his tongue.

When long fingers stretched the channel that was so hungry for him, she gasped, her knees going weak. But Nico was there to hold her up. His fingers moved back while his mouth took over. His lips nibbled at her clit, his tongue sweeping along her folds. Two fingers speared into her, moving lightly, setting up a rhythm that drove her nearly out of her mind. His other hand cupped her ass, the fingers sliding slowly toward the little hole secreted there.

Nico's magic fingers pushed against her back entrance and a whole different set of nerve endings flickered to life within her, coiling in her womb and causing untold heat to shimmer through her being.

"Come for me baby," Nico whispered against her clit. His warm breath and heated words washed over her, pushing her higher.

With a little gasping cry, she clenched around his hands, coming for him, at his command. Nico held her through the small peak, gently removing his hands only when she was over the crisis. He petted her, taking her in his arms and laying her on the big bed in the back of the wagon. He spread her out before him as if she belonged to him.

And she did.

Riki raised no objection when Nico climbed over her on the bed after discarding his clothes quickly. He spread her legs with his, coming down over her. His hard cock homed in on her pussy and lodged in the slick folds, apparently content to just rest there for now.

"I'm going to make you mine, Arikia. If you want me to stop, tell me now."

"Don't stop, Nico. I need you."

He smiled down at her, light shining from his hazel eyes. "As I need you, my heart, my love." Nico bent and kissed her, sliding his hard cock along the wet folds of her pussy, teasing, taunting, tempting her to take him inside. His lips trailed down over her neck, settling at her ripe breasts, driving her wild with need.

The fever rose higher and higher. Soon Riki was straining against him. She felt if he didn't take her soon, she might die of the wanting.

"Nico!" she cried out as he rose above her. "Please..."

Nico's gaze held hers as he pressed down and in, joining them by slow degrees. The pressure was relentless as he pushed inward, pulling back occasionally to ease his way. With each small give and take, he entered deeper, filling her with a sensation she'd never felt before.

Riki squeaked when the barrier was broken, but the pain was momentary. The pleasure and wonder of this man, this moment, overrode all. Nico was within her now, part of her, if only for these next few moments. She wished in her heart of hearts, she could keep him forever.

"It's done now." He leaned close to kiss her, resting within her for a quiet moment while she got used to the feeling.

But all too soon, she started to squirm. She needed something, though she didn't quite understand it. Her hips rolled, causing Nico to groan as he began to move. He pumped his hips slowly at first, holding her gaze, then more quickly as she met his thrusts with excited movements of her own.

Riki was burning up, the fire within rising higher and higher as Nico's thrusts became ever more powerful. He forged into her, sparking her senses as his hard cock claimed her in the most elemental way. Pain was forgotten. Shyness left aside. There was only this moment. This man.

"Nico!"

"We're almost there." His voice strained above her, a masculine growl from deep in his throat. "Come with me, Riki, come with me now."

Riki nearly lost consciousness as the wave of passion broke over her. She felt Nico tense inside her, his muscles going rigid against her skin as his cock erupted with streams of hot cum, filling her to overflowing. Riki reveled in the pleasure she could clearly read on his face as she found her own high peak, going to a place she'd never been before and hadn't even known existed.

Wrung out and utterly sated, Riki drifted down from the peak of pleasure to fall asleep in Nico's strong arms. He would keep her safe, she knew, both body and soul.

Riki woke much later, to softness, warmth and a feeling of immense security she had never felt before. Nico had her wrapped in his arms, spooning her from behind and she thought she'd never been more comfortable or content. Shifting slightly, she became aware of soreness in places she'd never been sore before and a flush stole up her neck.

"Is that blush for me, sweetheart?" Nico whispered in her ear a moment before burying his lips in her neck, tickling and sensually teasing at the same time. She squirmed and giggled, so unlike her usual somber self, enjoying the moment and the man. Nico pulled back and shifted, looking deep into her eyes. "How are you feeling this fine day?"

She felt the heat rise again in her cheeks as he grinned. "I'm a little sore."

"That's to be expected and I'm sorry for it, Riki, but I have to tell you—you made me the happiest man in the world last night. Thank you for your precious, selfless gift. I will treasure it—and you—always."

Riki caught her breath. Could he mean—?

"And was I right about your magic? Still there, right?"

His grin was endearing as Riki gasped. Taking quick stock, she found not only was the magic still part of her, it was stronger than before.

"It's there and it's...connected...to you." Wonder sounded in her voice, but he just smiled wider.

"We bonded a bit last night, sweetheart. It felt magnificent, didn't it? I hope you don't mind."

Mind? The thought raced through her brain. Nico didn't seem to be bothered by the idea that they could be bonded so closely. She was about to gather her courage to ask him if he might want more than just a short affair, when Drake banged loudly on the side of the wagon.

"Rise and shine, sleepyheads!" Drake's ebullient voice sounded from the other side of the small door to the wagon. "I have breakfast almost ready and then we need to be off. We have a long way to go today and no time to tarry."

Nico's knowing chuckle sent the blood creeping up her cheeks again, but he just kissed her and smiled.

"He knows?"

"Of course, he knows. The walls of this wagon are only thin planks of wood, after all." Nico sat up and began dressing, an all-too-pleased masculine smile on his face.

"You could've warned me." Riki tried hard to be angry with him, but she just felt too good to hold a grudge.

"I wouldn't have missed one single moan or breathless sigh for the world, sweetheart. Drake knows me well enough to tease me, but if he makes you uncomfortable, I'll tell him to bugger off."

Riki couldn't help but laugh at his cavalier attitude. Oh, he was in a fine mood this morning, and she felt some satisfaction for having put him there. She stood from the bed and threw on her dress.

"If he makes me uncomfortable, perhaps *I'll* tell him that." With a saucy grin, she headed for the door, only to be caught around the waist for a long, deep, satisfying kiss. Nico let her go eventually, and together they marched out to face the morning and Drake's teasing grin.

Chapter Eleven

Nico took the reins as they started on the road for the Jinnfaire. Breakfast had been a friendly, tasty affair. Drake was a good cook and an even better friend. He knew instinctively how far to go with his teasing and didn't cause Riki any undue embarrassment. For that, Nico would thank him later.

Drake wandered back into the wagon, emerging moments later with a few small musical instruments. Nico knew the bard would begin to test the limits of Riki's powers and help set some basic foundations to protect her, if he were right about her magical, musical gift.

"Do you play an instrument, milady?" Drake asked politely, as if simply curious.

"No," Riki replied wistfully and Nico could hear the longing in her voice. Perhaps Drake wasn't far off the mark in his suspicions about her gift. "I've always loved music, but have never had the opportunity to learn. Oh, I had a little tin whistle when I was a child, but that was long ago. My sister used to dance and I'd play a tune. I think it was called 'The Washerwoman'."

"Ah, I know that one." Drake launched into a complicated pattern on his small traveling lute, impressing even Nico with the dexterity of his fingers as they flew over the fret board.

"That's it!" Riki sounded breathless with excitement, reminding Nico of how she'd gasped his name in the night. But such thoughts were dangerous. He had to pay more attention to the road and less to the beguiling woman who had stolen his heart.

"As you can see, it's more suited to a whistle or pipe, but I can fake it on the lute as well."

As Nico drove the horses, Drake taught Riki the rudiments of both lute and hand drum. She was a natural, even Nico could tell, though he'd had to work very hard himself to master even the first few chords on the lute when he was taught as a child. Riki picked it up almost instantly, having a natural sense of rhythm and pitch that helped her immensely. Nico was duly impressed.

He was also impressed by the way she used her voice the few times Drake encouraged her to sing. No matter what she was singing, Nico was affected deeply by the words and moods of the selections. When she sang a lament, he felt as if his heart would break, when she sang a jig, he wanted to dance and sing along. And when she sang a fight song, he felt ready to take on Lucan and his entire army single-handed.

She could sway people with the magic of her voice, just like Drake had claimed. Nico became a believer during that long ride, as Drake put her through her paces, all without ever pushing her or letting her realize she was being tested. Drake's pointedly raised eyebrows spoke eloquently to Nico of the depth of their discovery. Riki had a powerful gift that impressed even Drake, who was used to such things. That alone brought home the importance of her gift to Nico.

As twilight rolled over the land and barren rock gave way to alpine trees, Drake indicated they were nearing their destination. They traveled a bit more slowly then, watching for the challenge Drake assured them would soon come.

The trees grew thicker and the road more narrow, when suddenly their path was blocked.

"Who seeks to enter here?" A Jinn warrior materialized out of the mist. Nico stopped the wagon, but it was Drake who took the lead, standing in the seat to put himself between any possible arrow and Riki, who was still in the back of the wagon.

"Drake of the Five Lands," he announced in a strong voice.

"And who is this with you?"

"I am Nick, Swordmaster of Melnibown, Swordsinger of Eastbourne, Knifemaster of Westerdown... Shall I go on?" A raised eyebrow challenged the Jinn warrior who was smiling now, widely.

"I have heard of those three men. Interesting to see them all before me claiming to be one person. Can you prove your titles?"

Before the soldier could blink, a knife thunked into the ground at his feet. He bent to pick it up, then threw it straight at Nico, but he was prepared. Shifting lightly, he raised his hands and caught the flying knife between them, without flinching, evading or drawing a single drop of blood. Nico held up his uninjured palms to show the man, then sheathed the knife back into its hidden resting place over his chest.

"Well met, Blademaster," the Jinn warrior finally conceded. "I am Zachari. I lead the warriors of the Black Dragon Clan. You will be welcome among our people for Drake's sake and your own."

"There is another. Possibly, the One we seek." A woman's voice rang through the mist-shrouded trees off to the side of the track. "Bring her forward." A tall, raven-haired woman strode from the trees. She was stunning and had emerald green eyes.

She wore the gold jewelry of her Clan, a pendant shaped into a dragon, wings stretched in flight. Nico's gaze lit upon it and he smiled, despite the demand to see Riki.

"You have a woman with you?" Zachari demanded, looking from Drake to Nico and back again.

"She's mine," Nico growled, making his possession clear.

But the woman raised her eyebrow, grinning at him slyly. "Isn't that for her to decide?"

A hand on his back urged Nico to stand aside so Riki could make her way out from the back of the wagon. Nico jumped down and offered his hand to help her alight. Bravely, she faced the other woman. She was shorter and thinner than the voluptuous black-haired beauty, but they both had a regal bearing that was unmistakable. Nico was never prouder of her than in that moment.

"I'm Riki," she said simply. "Nico's mate."

The dragon inside him roared while Nico took Riki's hand in his and raised it to his lips. How he loved her! His brave, beautiful mate.

Turning back to the Jinn, Nico was shocked to see both Zachari and the woman lower themselves to one knee before them. Riki looked similarly surprised, allowing Nico to pull her backward, into his embrace as they waited to see what was afoot.

"Friends, what means this?" Drake spoke into the silence.

The woman looked up and smiled, though tears leaked down her face. "We welcome you, Arikia, the one who was foretold. We've long awaited your arrival."

"How do you know my name?" Riki breathed.

The woman laughed. "The Jinn have ways of knowing. We of the Black Dragon Clan have our own additional methods of learning things...cousin."

"Cousin?" Riki was clearly confused, as was Nico.

In answer, the woman chuckled, raising her arms as a black mist enveloped her body. Within moments, she stood before them—a black dragon. Nico felt the threat she posed and without thought transformed himself, facing down the female black who threatened his mate.

The Jinn warrior jumped back and suddenly a legion of Jinn soldiers emerged from the trees to surround the wagon and the two black dragons who now eyed each other warily. They faced off, tension clear in every line of their sleek bodies, each unsure of the other's motives, until a small, brave woman strode between them. Riki.

She put her small hand on Nico's scaled knee, the connection comforting even as he watched the other dragon. He had no idea of this startling woman's intentions. But no one shifted to dragon form without good reason.

Riki faced the dragon-woman bravely. "Please, can we talk about this as humans? We have no idea what's going on here and we need to understand."

The tension diffused as the woman shifted back to human form. Nico followed suit, though he still eyed her warily. But the woman only smiled.

"You, then, are our cousin as well. Be welcome, Prince Nicolas, and forgive me for alarming you. I have dreamed of this day. We have all dreamed of this day." She gestured to the warriors watching all around. "I am Estella, Steward of the Black Dragon Clan."

"You can shift," Riki observed with wonder.

"Of course, can't you?"

Sadly, Riki shook her head. “I don’t think so.”

But Estella only laughed. “Don’t worry, little cousin. It comes to females later than males.”

“Really?” Riki looked so hopeful, Nico hated to get her hopes up in case this startling woman was wrong.

“Enter and be welcome, dragon-cousins. Now I understand why the seer guided us to include Drake among the Brotherhood. He was the instrument that would lead us to you. Thank you, Drake.” She turned to Drake, who had also come down off the wagon when the warriors appeared, and kissed him soundly. “We are again in your debt. Come, let us find comfort. Zachari, have your men take the horses and wagon while I show our new friends to the camp.”

Riki was startled to find an entire city of brightly colored tents as they emerged from the line of trees. She felt a tingle against her skin that warned her magic was in the air. No other way could this many people and tents remain hidden, she reasoned. The Jinn were rumored to have a great deal of magic and Riki could easily see and feel the rumors were true. She had always been sensitive to the use of magic and her senses had only grown more acute as Loralie had done her dastardly work with Lucan.

Each time the North Witch used her power, Riki had felt it like a blow to her senses. Dark and evil magic was what skiths thrived on and the feel of it tainted all they touched. But this Jinn magic was pure and bright. It felt happy and it welcomed Riki like the arms of a mother. She felt Nico bristle next to her and put her hand out to hold his.

“Don’t worry, Nico,” she said softly. “We’re among friends. I can tell.”

Are you certain? She knew he spoke in her mind to avoid detection and realized it was a good idea.

I can feel the magic of this place and these people. It isn't evil. They have no evil intent toward us. At least not right now. I would feel it if they did.

Truly? Nico sounded skeptical and she moved to reassure him.

Yes, truly. Having spent so much time around Lucan, don't you think I'd recognize evil magic if it faced us? I've felt it on our trail from time to time, but this isn't it. In fact, this is protective magic. Nothing can harm us here.

Estella led them to a large, central tent in one section of the huge encampment, inviting them in with a flourish and a warm smile. The woman was gorgeous and she could shift to dragon form too. Riki felt a pang, wondering if Nico would prefer Estella to her. It was clear the woman was much more accomplished than she was.

"Sit here, please, and I'll have food and wine brought in. I know your road has been long to find us, as has ours to find you. The seer will want to speak with you, I know, and I'm sure you have many questions. Just give me a minute to arrange things."

Estella left the tent and the three of them were alone for a few moments.

"What do you think?" Drake asked quietly.

"Riki seems to think there's magic in the air and I'm inclined to agree." Nico pulled her hand into his lap as they sat at a low table.

"But it's good magic," Riki insisted. "Not evil. They use it to hide their encampment, for one thing. I felt it as we walked through the barrier, didn't you?"

Drake shook his head, blue eyes wide. Nico seemed to consider before responding. "I felt a kind of tingle, but shrugged it off. Was that the barrier?"

"Probably. It felt like a million butterfly wings tickling against my skin." She smiled at the memory. "It was friendly and benign."

"At least to you." A new voice sounded from the entrance to the tent. In the doorway stood a stately older woman in long, colorful robes. She walked with a slight limp as she moved toward the table and the men rose in respect until she was seated across from Riki. "I am the seer, Arabetta. Welcome, Arikia, daughter of Adora, descendant of Kent. I have awaited your arrival these many years."

"You see the future?" Nico asked softly, his eyes measuring.

"Sometimes," the woman shrugged. "Not always in enough time to do anything about what I see, or I would have sent men to prevent the murder of your parents, Prince Nicolas. Please accept my apologies and condolences. Your father was a great man and a true friend to the Jinn. Sadly, the connection was lost when he died, for your brother Roland knew nothing of our bonds, nor did any of the other royal princes. It's taken us years to reestablish the link that should never have been lost. You, Sir Drake, have been instrumental in that, and for that great service, I thank you."

Riki looked over at Drake. He looked as if he might object to the old woman calling him "sir". After all, he was the son of knights, not a knight himself, but just then Estella returned, bringing with her a troop of people with platters of food and flasks of wine. They set them on the wide table and looked over the new arrivals with open curiosity. They placed the items mostly in front of Riki as if seeking her approval. She made a point to smile and thank everyone who sought her eye, flushing a little with the strange attention, but impressed by the friendly eagerness of these people.

Estella sat next to the seer and began to pour out the wine. When she was finished, she raised her cup. "To the Mother of All with many thanks for reuniting the black dragons on this day. Blessed be the Mother of All."

"Blessed be." The others repeated the words and Riki followed suit, raising her cup of wine and drinking with the rest of them. The wine was fruity and delicious, tartly zapping Riki's tongue and making her smile.

"This is delicious."

"I'm glad you like it," Estella topped up her cup before sitting back and lifting some roasted meat from a platter. "Please eat. We'll talk while you refresh yourselves with a meal."

"Are you the only black dragon here?" Nico asked quickly.

Estella chuckled. "No, Prince Nicolas. We of the Black Dragon Clan are descended of Jintau, the youngest son of Draneth the Wise. He had many children. It was they who founded the Jinn Brotherhood generations ago. Since then, the Jinn have spread out all over the lands, but the black dragons remain the core of the Jinn. Our clan rules all the other clans, and only our clan has the ability to shift. Among our clan, we have perhaps a dozen younger dragons and several elders who do not do much flying these days."

"You're one of those," Riki said astutely, her eyes on the seer.

Arabetta nodded. "Sadly, when one reaches a certain age, flying is something that can be painful as well as uplifting. I don't fly much anymore, but I can still do so if needed."

"Amazing." Nico's whisper brought a smile to the older woman's eyes.

The seer nodded her head with a gentle smile. “I must tell you of the danger I have foreseen, Prince Nicolas. It concerns all the lands, but most especially Draconia.”

That got the attention of everyone at the table. They waited for the older woman to continue.

“There is a place, far in the northland wastes, known only as the Citadel. It was to this place the last of the wizards sealed their enemies and set a caretaker to watch over their resting place. It is to the Citadel, Lucan prepares to go. You must stop him before he succeeds in waking the sleeping wizards trapped there or our lands will know terror the likes of which we have not seen since the Wizard Wars.”

“I’ve been taught about the Citadel, Lady, but I thought it was only legend.” Nico regarded the older woman with respect and a bit of awe.

“Oh, the Citadel is real enough, as is the hereditary caretaker, though the caretaker’s powers have grown weaker with each successive generation. It is all the current caretaker can do to stem the tide and she has made some...unwise choices on her path as she fought to keep the secret of the Citadel safe.” Arabetta sighed. “But the time is coming soon when we will all be tested. Dragons, humans, and others will unite to hopefully prevent a catastrophe beyond which even I cannot see. The fate of our world lies in the balance. You must leave soon for your homeland. Your brother and his mate must be made aware of what is coming. And you will take with you an honor guard of emissaries from the Jinn to Draconia. Our time of hiding is over. The Black Dragon Clan will fight alongside our cousins in Draconia. You must tell your brother that as well.”

“I will. Thank you, Lady Arabetta.” Nico’s voice was formal and somewhat subdued. “I cannot say how glad I am to find the black dragons will rally together. The dragons of my land will be heartened to know the line of Draneth continues to grow strong, even outside the borders of our land. You will all be welcome among us."

"Well spoken, Prince Nicolas. But there is one thing that must transpire before you can return to your home." The old woman looked from Nico, pointedly to Riki and back. "You must marry our new queen."

"Queen?" Riki could hardly believe her ears. "What in the world?"

"It was foreseen generations ago that a daughter of Kent would come to us, to unite the Black Dragon Clan with our allies. The leadership of the Black Dragon Clan has ever been only a stewardship. Estella's line holds authority over affairs of state until such time as the daughter of Kent came to us. The leadership of the Black Dragon Clan is at least partly yours, Arikia. Our system was designed so the queen rules over diplomatic affairs, and her steward deals with tribal matters. It has ever been thus, from the beginning."

"But that's impossible! I'm not even Jinn. And I can't shift." She was near tears as all eyes focused on her.

"You have the soul of a dragon, child. That is all that is required to be Jinn. As for shifting, it will come—or not—in time. In truth, it makes no difference. You are the One who was foretold. You are the One we will follow into battle. Other than that, Jinn royalty serves little purpose, if truth be told, since we are a mostly scattered people. Perhaps that will make you feel better." The old woman chuckled. "Regardless, our queen you shall be. As it was foretold."

Estella spoke up, her warm voice gentle and sure. "Bloodlines are very important to the Jinn. Jintau married Jora, a princess from Elderland in the far east. In that land, even today, men are protectors and warriors, but the women rule.

That is how Jora designed the Jinn. She ruled over her many children and their mates, plus the other displaced peoples who came to them to form the Jinn Brotherhood. Jora was a strong seer and foretold of this time in great detail. She knew her children would lead the Jinn in battle, but she also knew it would take new blood to reunite the Jinn with the other children of Draneth."

"Draneth himself, it is said, counseled his youngest son to follow Jora's vision." Arabetta nodded wisely as she stated her belief, but Riki could hardly believe what these women were saying. It seemed so ridiculous. So impossible.

Nico's hand found hers, grasping tightly, lending her his strength. *Say nothing yet, sweetheart. Let's see where this leads, all right?*

She looked up into his eyes and fed on his surety of purpose, his strength and his conviction. These people were important for their safety and for the safety of all the dragons and people of Draconia. Riki would not let them down out of fear. She'd take Nico's advice and see what these people wanted of her before giving in to the fear threatening even now, to overwhelm her.

I need you to help me, Nico. I'm afraid. Admitting that was one of the hardest things she'd ever done, but Nico was her rock. He would help her. She knew it in her soul, when she would never have said such words, or admitted such weakness, to anyone else in the world.

Nico squeezed her hand. *I will always be here for you, Riki. I will always be at your side, ready to catch you. Don't be afraid. Together we can handle anything.*

Tears gathered behind her eyes, but she refused to let them fall. Summoning her courage, fortified by Nico's support, she faced the Jinn women.

"I don't understand any of this, but I'm willing to listen."

Arabetta beamed at her. "Spoken like a true queen."

Riki felt pride at the woman's apparent confidence in her, but it was tempered with fear and bewilderment. How could these people really think she was a queen? Didn't they know she was a coward?

"Now to the marriage," Estella said briskly, shocking Riki back to the strange conversation.

"Bloodlines are all important among the Jinn. That is something that's been passed down from Jora and her Elderland beliefs. You two must marry in our traditions for your union to be fully recognized, and you must do it now, before you leave for Draconia."

"But—" Riki was cut off by the old woman.

"I know you'd rather have a big ceremony. What bride doesn't want that? But we cannot afford the time. We've already begun preparations for a feast tonight, preceded of course, by the joining ceremony."

"But—"

"One of our finest tailors is preparing a wedding dress for you as we speak."

"But—"

"The minstrels are preparing their best songs and representatives of all the Jinn clans are gathering from every corner. This is the largest Jinnfaire in a hundred years. As many as possible have come to witness your joining."

Riki shouted to be heard, her frustration building as the old woman rode right over all her objections. "But he hasn't asked me to marry him!"

Dead silence greeted her outburst and frowns were directed at Nico from every corner, raising her protective instincts.

"Don't you look at him like that," she scolded. "We only just met a few days ago. How could anyone expect a man to fall in love in so short a time?"

"But a woman could, couldn't she?" Drake's knowing words caused heat to rush to her cheeks.

"That isn't the point of this discussion." She pointedly ignored Nico, afraid of what she might see on his face.

But Nico tugged on her hand, demanding she face him. *I knew you were mine the first moment I saw you, my love. The dragon in me recognized its mate from the beginning. I do love you, my Arikia, and I want you to be my wife, my lover, my mate for life. Will you consent? Do you love me, even a little?*

His words, for her alone, touched her deeply. She raised her gaze slowly to look at his beautiful face and the tender expression in his hazel eyes nearly made her cry. She saw love shining from his eyes—and this wasn't the first time, if she were being honest with herself. No, but this was the first time he'd spoken the words plainly.

She reached out, practically throwing herself into his arms. "I love you so much!" she whispered into his ear before pulling back and kissing him soundly.

Nico deepened the kiss, lifting her right off the seat and onto his lap as he devoured her mouth. Riki's senses spun with the wonder of him and his words of love. She felt the bands stretching from her soul to his strengthen and she knew without being told, of his deep and true affection. She could feel it. Just as he could probably feel echoes of her feelings for him.

When he drew back, she was pressed against his chest, her bottom seated snugly in his lap and his smile stretched from ear to ear. There was a tenderness in his gaze she had only ever seen when he looked at her and she knew it now for what it was...love.

"Will you be my bride, Arikia?" His tender tone left her breathless.

"Yes, Nico," she whispered, lost in his hazel green gaze.

"About time," Arabetta groused good-naturedly, reminding Riki starkly that they had an audience. She tried to straighten, but Nico's arms held her tight against him.

"Forgive me, Lady," Nico addressed the old woman. "Riki has not had the easiest life and I wanted to give her time to adjust to me. I didn't want to scare off my true mate by acting too soon."

Arabetta's frown cleared. "You are far wiser than I gave you credit for, Prince Nicolas. I beg your pardon."

The shock on Estella's face showed just how surprising the old seer's words were to her and Riki felt some satisfaction the woman would admit to being wrong about Nico. He was as close to perfect as a man could be, after all. Riki hugged the knowledge of his love to her heart and crowed like a child inside, where none could hear. Nico loved her and wanted to marry her. It was a miracle of light in her formerly dark, sad, desolate world. Nico brought joy and happiness to her when she thought she would never know it again...and love. He brought her love when she'd despaired of ever feeling such tender emotions for a man in her life. *He* was a miracle.

Nico nodded, accepting the woman's apology without comment, letting the moment pass naturally. He was a good diplomat, Riki realized with pride.

"I'd planned to marry in Draconia, once we returned, but if you say the Jinn must be satisfied—and Riki is willing—I'm happy to do so here. The sooner we are joined in the eyes of all, the happier I will be." He leaned down to kiss her temple, holding her close in his strong arms. Riki felt cherished for the first time in many, many long years.

Chapter Twelve

The wedding ceremony was like nothing Riki had ever seen or even expected. She realized she'd given up on the idea of marrying or finding love sometime during her imprisonment. She'd lost hope for any kind of future at all, but Nico had returned it to her.

She went into the ceremony without any reservations. Certainly, Riki was astounded by the lovely green silk dress the tailor had made for her. The green was the exact color of her eyes and the skirt swirled around her legs in feather soft caresses that nearly made her giddy. There were layers to go underneath as well, also in silk, but pale green and gold this time.

Riki had been brought to a private tent to prepare. Several women helped her, all of whom had green eyes like hers, and claimed to be cousins of one sort or another. They'd prepared a steaming bath, scented with rare gardenias from the southlands. The fragrance was intoxicating and the rich soap they gave her to wash and lotions for her hair were of the finest quality she had ever used.

Riki was overwhelmed by the Jinn women's generosity. They helped her dress, showing her what pieces went where and laughing at her shy attempts to figure them out on her own. They were kind to her and their welcome nearly reduced her to tears several times, but then one of the women would start singing a happy tune and her mood would lighten.

When she was suitably dressed and prepared, the women brought her to a large clearing in the center of the encampment. There were hundreds, perhaps thousands of people standing all around a raised platform. As they drew closer, she could see Nico and Drake waiting on top of the platform, watching as she came forward. Somewhere a group of minstrels struck up a tune that carried through the happy crowd and smiles lit each and every face.

Riki's nerves faded away to nothing when she saw Nico there, waiting for her. Eagerly, she climbed the make-shift steps, holding out one hand to Nico as she drew closer. He not only took her hand but pulled her in close for a quick hug. The crowd cheered loudly and she moved back, a little embarrassed to be in front of so many people, but their song was so happy, it did away with most of her fears.

Arabetta strode forward with several other Jinn elders, all standing with them on the large platform. The crowd grew quiet and the song faded away, leaving joy in its wake. Arabetta stopped in front of Riki and Nico, facing them.

"Who stands witness for this joining?" the old woman asked formally.

"I stand for the bride." Estella moved next to Riki, smiling as she took a place at her side.

"And I stand for the groom." Drake spoke from Nico's side.

Arabetta nodded and began to sing. Or perhaps chant would be a better word, Riki thought, as she felt the magic of Arabetta's voice like a living thing. This was powerful magic, indeed, channeled through the ancient words. Riki didn't understand the ancient tongue, but the meaning was clear. She actually felt ethereal bands of magic swirling around herself and Nico, twining them together where their hands were still joined, up and around both of their bodies and souls.

When the chant ended there was an expectant hush in the air.

Arabetta turned to Riki.

“Do you, Arikia, promise your heart and soul to Nicolas?”

Not knowing what else to say, Riki opted for simply saying, “I do.”

Then Arabetta turned to Nico.

“Do you, Nicolas, promise your heart and soul to Arikia?”

“I do,” he stated in a firm voice, leaving no doubt as to his strong intent.

“Then kiss and be one.”

The crowd cheered as Nico bent to kiss her, taking her in his muscular arms. The noise of the crowd faded away as Nico sealed their promises with a binding kiss. Riki felt the magic twining them together, joining their magics and making them more powerful. It was an amazing feeling, and like nothing she’d ever experienced before.

When Nico released finally her some time later, the crowd was singing and cheering happily. Arabetta looked at them both expectantly.

“It is customary among Jinn to wear rings of marriage. The ones we arranged for Drake to acquire in Plinth were made especially for you two. They are plain enough for a spy on the outside, but if you look inside the bands, they bear the mark of the Black Dragon Clan. Welcome to the Brotherhood of the Jinn. We’ve been long awaiting you both.”

Arabetta hugged first Riki, then Nico and the congratulations spread from there. Riki was hugged and congratulated by all the people on the platform, including

Estella and Drake. As they made their way off the platform, she and Nico were bombarded with well-wishes from everyone near them.

Estella led them to a private tent where a large dinner was laid out, ready and waiting. Estella and Drake were the only ones to join them, which surprised Riki. The sounds of revelry could be clearly heard through the thin tent walls.

Drake sat with Estella on one side of the low table. Colorful cushions were spread all around. This tent was different from the other Jinn tents Riki had been in. For one thing, this tent had few furnishings besides the low table and a multitude of pillows. There were ropes hanging in one corner, though Riki could see no use for them. Likewise, she didn't understand some of the other odd accoutrements on the table.

Estella began eating from the sumptuous feast before them and something about her manner piqued Riki's interest. Some deeper game was being played here, but she had no idea what it was.

"So how did you like your Jinn wedding ceremony?" Estella's eyes sparkled as she nibbled on a fruit in a way that made Riki think of nibbling on Nico. She didn't know why, but that's what she immediately thought of, and it shocked her a bit. And excited her.

"I thought it was beautiful, actually." Riki accepted the plate of delicacies Nico set before her with a smile. He was so thoughtful, and the fire in his eyes promised a passionate night ahead.

"Short and sweet, then we get to the good part," Drake agreed with a laugh from the other side of the low table. "Nick, I have to thank you for choosing me as a witness." Drake leered playfully at Estella and Riki got the impression there was something more to this witnessing business than just standing before the elders with the bride and groom.

"What does that entail, exactly?" she asked boldly.

Estella and Drake chuckled naughtily while Nico narrowed his eyes at them both. Riki knew he would protect her from anything she was uncomfortable with, Jinn tradition or no. That knowledge gave her the courage to press the issue. She waited expectantly for an answer and finally Estella seemed to take pity on her.

"The witnesses stand before the elders. We also ensure your first joining as man and wife goes smoothly."

"And that you fuck like bunnies until morning," Drake put in, earning an elbow to the ribs from Estella.

"The Jinn tend to marry very young. Having witnesses is meant to help the younger couples, who are often virgins. Most often, the witnesses are a married couple who guide the youngsters on the path. How much they participate is up to the individual couple being joined." Estella shrugged. "Since your Nico chose Drake—an unmarried man of some rank—to be his witness, it was only logical I stand for you. Drake and I have shared pleasure before."

Riki was shocked by the casual way Estella spoke of such private acts. True, she'd seen all kinds of things as Lucan's prisoner, but this wasn't deviant in the way Lucan had been. There was no pain or suffering involved here—just the sharing of pleasure for mutual enjoyment. She could even see how an inexperienced couple might find solace from having friends there to help them.

But Nico was far from inexperienced and having already been his lover, Riki didn't think she needed any help from either Estella or Drake, though having them watch did sound exciting. Riki remembered that time in Drake's room at the Silver

Serpent when Nico had invited his handsome friend to touch her and look at her while Nico pleasured her. It had been wild, exotic, and incredibly erotic. Riki had learned then, she liked being watched.

"There is also the fact that sometimes among the Black Dragon Clan, a wedding night could include a mating flight," Estella went on as she continued to enjoy her supper. "Especially when dealing with young dragons, the older ones stand by ready to catch them if they fall too far, too fast. But we don't have to worry about that tonight, since you can't fly yet."

Riki liked the confident way Estella said "yet", but Riki doubted she'd ever be able to shift into dragon form. That was a dream for another time.

Nico moved close to her, taking her hand and bringing it to his lips. *If you don't want them here, just say the word, my love. I don't give a damn if it's Jinn tradition or not. We do what we want, and all I want is your happiness and comfort.*

Riki stroked his cheek, smiling up at him. *I love you so much, Nico. Would you be shocked if I said I was...intrigued by the idea of having them watch?*

No, love, it wouldn't surprise me at all. We dragons are exhibitionists at heart.

Nico chuckled as he lay her hand in his lap, directly over his steely erection, leaving her to eat with only her right hand. She didn't mind at all.

"Oh look, they're already making gooey eyes at each other." Drake snorted as he threw one arm around Estella's shoulder.

"You be nice, Drake," she warned. "They're in love. Don't you remember what that's like?"

Drake seemed to think about the question, a light entering his eyes that made Riki feel a sudden and sweeping sympathy for the rogue. He looked so lost in that moment, it stunned her, but then he smiled, wiping the distressing expression from his face. Playfully, he tugged Estella into his lap.

"I don't claim to ever have been in love, sweet."

"That is so sad." Estella teased him as she cupped his cheek and planted a hot kiss on his agile lips. Riki got hot just watching.

Do you like watching them? Nico's voice sounded through her mind. *They are a handsome couple, don't you think?*

Yes, they are.

Shall we watch them as they watch us? Or should we ask them to join us perhaps? What's your pleasure, milady?

Riki was torn. She didn't know what she wanted. She only knew her temperature was rising with each sweep of Drake's tongue into Estella's mouth. Drake's hands were busy too, roving over Estella's voluptuous figure, removing her clothing while she tore at his.

What about it, sweet? What do you want? Nico asked again.

Whatever you want, Nico. I'll do whatever you say.

Oh, I like the sound of that, but remember, my love, if anything makes you uncomfortable at any time, all you have to do is tell me.

All right, Nico.

He kissed her then, sweeping his tongue inside her mouth and taking her down into the nest of pillows behind the low table. Nico worked at her clothing until Riki was bare, all the while kissing her as if he would never get enough of her sweet taste.

Nico craved Riki like his next breath. He worked the buttons on the beautiful dress with eager fingers, wanting to feel her skin on his with an urgency he'd never felt before. This woman was his now in every possible way.

The dragon inside him trumpeted in triumph while the man fumbled with little buttons and feminine undergarments, all designed to drive him crazy. He heard a tear and knew he had to slow down. The dragon was urging him to take and claim his mate in the rough way of their kind, but Riki was human too, and she needed him to be tender.

Especially in this new situation.

Nico had fucked his share of women. Hell, he'd even shared a woman or two in his youth with Drake and others, but even though Estella was more than just pretty, Nico only felt real attraction for his new wife. He finally understood what his friends had gone through when they'd found their mates. He finally knew the wonder of claiming the one woman whom you would love and honor for the rest of your days.

"I told you they didn't need any help from us."

Drake's teasing words penetrated Nico's mind as if from far away. Nico looked up to find his grinning friend and a very naked Estella smiling down at them.

"Go away. Can't you see I'm busy here?" Nico growled before turning back to his wife.

Wife.

She really was his wife now, in the eyes of the Jinn at least, which was good enough for him. The Jinn, like most Draconians, believed in the Mother of All and had joined them before Her. That was enough. Riki was well and truly his wife now. Nico still couldn't believe his good fortune.

"So you're in a hurry then?" Drake continued to annoy him. "I thought we'd give some of the toys in this tent a try, just for the sake of completeness."

The reminder of the way the Jinn had equipped this particular tent for them lit a fire in his belly. Nico held Riki's gaze as he removed the last of her clothing and sat up. "That's the best idea you've had all night, Drake."

When Drake didn't answer, Nico looked around to find his friend had already moved to the corner with the ropes. At that moment, he was busy tying up the lovely and very cooperative Estella. Her fleshy ass faced them as Drake smiled over to make sure they were watching. He smacked Estella's butt cheeks with a loud clap of his palm and she squealed, but it wasn't in pain.

Riki jumped in Nico's arms and he soothed her, bending close to lick her ear. Nico knew some of this might be hard for her considering the things she'd probably witnessed with Lucan, but the goal here was to free her of those past horrors. She needed to see how pleasure could come of safe, sane play between consenting adults. Drake was just the man to demonstrate while Nico explained to his new wife all the possibilities. Knowing she was half-dragon, he knew the rougher edge of sex would more than likely be what she needed. Nico gauged her reaction, watching the flare of her eyes and the increase in her breathing. She was excited—not scared—and it would be up to him to keep her that way.

"Sometimes a spanking can be very enticing," he whispered in her ear.

"Really?" The word was a breathy whisper as Drake's hand came down on Estella's ass once more, followed by the Jinn woman's feminine moan of pleasure.

"It can be a loving give and take of dominance and submission. Among dragons, the male dominates his partner in the mating flight. They say the female revels in her mate's power as he does in her submission. It's the way of things." He licked a trail down her neck. "For dragons."

Drake was more aggressive now, interspersing stokes of Estella's generous curves with slaps to her ass and thighs. The Jinn woman moaned and begged for Drake to continue his sensuous torture, clearly loving every minute of it.

"I'm half dragon, my love, as are you. Don't you want to submit to me in every way? Doesn't your inner dragon long to be mastered by mine?"

Riki's breath caught in her throat, her eyes mesmerized by the most erotic thing she'd ever witnessed. Nico's hands and words inflamed her senses while Drake's mastery of the Jinn woman was titillating her desire.

She hadn't realized this kind of play could be anything but painful. What she'd seen in Lucan's chamber had been a cruel mockery of the sensual, seductive, sinuous dance of dominance she now witnessed. Drake demonstrated his total control of Estella's freely given responses and Riki began to wonder what it would be like to surrender so completely and utterly to the man she loved.

Nico's question bounced around in her brain. Dare she admit how hot the thought made her? Would he hurt her if he knew he could have anything he wanted from her? Anything at all?

The answer shouted through her mind—an immediate, resounding no. Nico would never hurt her. He was her mate. The dragon that shared her soul knew Nico and wanted nothing more than to submit to him fully. Riki found her human side wanted the same thing. She wanted to learn all he could teach her of pleasure and passion.

Nico's hands tightened. One hand clamped her waist, the other squeezing a nipple. Riki squirmed in his hold, more excited than she'd ever been.

"Don't you want to surrender, my Arikia? Answer me."

Riki moaned as he pinched her nipple just hard enough to send a flame shooting from the taut peak straight to her womb. She was on fire!

"I do. I surrender to you, Nico. Only to you."

He turned her in his arms, dragging her close against his body. Nico kissed her hungrily, invading her mouth and asserting a dominance he'd heretofore held in check. She wanted it all now. She wanted his dominance, his roughness, his daring.

And he gave it to her.

Drake and Estella were forgotten as Nico took her to the floor, covering her straining body with his own. She fought with the ties on his leggings, wanting—no, needing—more of him, all of him. And suddenly he was there, as naked as she, as vulnerable. Nico was the master of her passion, the master of her heart. His strong body covered her, his eyes holding hers as he joined them as one.

And then it was done.

Bodies met, souls met, more fully than ever before. Riki's complete submission joined them fully. Rather than tearing her down and being consumed by his dominant personality, it felt more like Nico's power flowed into and around her, cupping her in warm arms of energy, holding her safe and urging her to fly with him.

Riki saw into his soul through the hazel green fire in his eyes and she knew he was seeing into hers as well. They were one now, in all ways.

Then he began to move.

The slow dance of seduction and pleasure quickly turned to an inferno neither wanted to tamp down. Nico took her hard and fast, almost brutally, but she wanted every inch of his domination, every surge of his powerful body and spirit. She was his as he was hers.

The powerful climax hit them both at the same time, Nico gasping as Riki cried out in ultimate pleasure. It was a hard, fast climb to an unbelievable pinnacle, over too soon, but necessary to join what would never be put apart again.

"I love you, my Arikia, my wife." Nico whispered in her ear as they both had a chance to recover.

"I know," Riki said softly, loving the feel of him on her and in her. "As much as I love you."

He kissed her then, a tender, powerful claiming, affirming what they both knew in their hearts, now beating as one.

Riki must have dozed a bit, for when she woke it was to the sound of feminine whimpers of pleasure. Opening her eyes, Riki found herself on Nico's lap, her bare thighs spread over his outstretched knees, facing Drake and Estella. The other couple had left the corner of the colorful tent and the ropes, in favor of a matted area closer by. Drake had Estella on all fours, his long cock taking her powerfully from behind.

"What do you think?" Nico asked, his warm breath tickling her ear. "They look good together, don't they?"

Riki nodded as she watched them. Drake's powerful blond good looks were a perfect foil for Estella's dark haired beauty and curvy body. They were beautiful together, and if there was no deep and true love tying them together, there was at the very least respect and friendship. That much was obvious from the way they teased and tempted each other. They moved together like long-time lovers and Riki realized they probably were.

Nico moved one hand to the low table behind them. Moving his arm in front of her once more, Riki saw he now held a long, thick object she'd thought was some kind of ornament for the table. Only now did she realize the shape of this colorful glass object was almost exactly that of a cock. Her insides quivered as Nico's hot breath breezed over her neck.

"This was a wedding gift from Estella. Her brother is Master Glasswright of the Black Dragon Clan." Nico bit down on her earlobe. "She showed me some of the other gifts the Jinn sent us earlier while you were getting dressed. These folks are naughty with a penchant for sexual toys. I'll take great pleasure in showing some of the more adventurous ones to you when we're alone, but for now, I thought you might like to try this." He moved the smooth, colorful glass to her mouth. "Lick it, sweetheart. Make it slick and warm with your tongue."

Riki felt the fire inside leap at his words. Slowly, she reached out with the tip of her tongue, accepting the smooth head of the glass cock into her mouth as Nico maneuvered it slowly, sliding it in and out like he would slide his own cock. The thought sent her senses reeling. A moment later, the glass dildo was sliding wetly down her torso, heading toward her pussy and she shivered with excitement. Would he—?

Yes, apparently he would.

The glass cock entered her, cold at first, slick and getting slicker by the moment with her heated juices. It felt odd, hard and unyielding, but exciting. Nico moved it inside her, manipulating it to reach spots within her core that set her ablaze. She whimpered as he began to thrust the glass cock in and out, her temperature going higher when she looked up and saw Drake's blue gaze locked on the area between her legs.

Drake was buried balls deep in Estella, his hard-muscled body straining as he watched Nico pleasure Riki with the glass cock. The idea of him watching titillated and when Drake came, so did Riki, in a little explosion of light she knew would build into something much more fierce if Nico was given just half a chance.

Nico turned her, bringing her to the floor and spreading her wide while he positioned her just so. A quick glance told him Drake was sitting cross-legged, petting Estella, who was smiling in that sleepy, satisfied way that meant she'd come long and hard under Drake's skillful attentions.

Nico looked his fill at his woman. His wife. Arikia. She was so beautiful, so eager, and with him every step of the way. He wondered if he couldn't push her limits just a little further while he had Drake handy. Who knew when this opportunity would arise again?

With a glance, he summoned the other man over.

Riki's eyes widened when Drake knelt at her side, but the fire of excitement leapt within and Nico could feel the energy sizzling through their connection. She was ready for what he had in store. Ready, willing and more than able.

"Drake, would you be so kind as to play with this," he indicated the glass dildo, still embedded in Riki's wet pussy, "while my woman sucks my cock?"

Drake smiled widely as he moved around Riki's squirming body. "It would be my pleasure." He licked his lips. "Hers too."

Nico hesitated a moment before turning over the base of the glass rod to his friend. Drake was a rascal, but Nico knew he could be trusted. Nico moved away and watched Riki's response as Drake settled on his haunches between her spread thighs.

All right? He sent on their private path of communication.

She nodded, shivering as Drake began manipulating the dildo, shafting it in and out of her hot body. *Come to me, Nico. I need you.*

He could wait no more. Nico took up a position next to her head, raising her just slightly with some of the colorful pillows supporting her back. She knew just what he liked, taking his cock between her luscious lips as if savoring a special treat. He felt the swirling action of her tongue down to his very toes. Stars, what a woman!

And she was all his. Forevermore.

Nico's eyes closed, savoring the feel of her eager mouth. She jerked and his eyes shot open only to find his rogue of a friend was now licking Riki's clit, eyes smiling up at him from between his wife's legs. The bastard.

Nico shook his head and laughed. Give Drake an inch and he always took a mile. It was one thing they had in common. He should be mad, but Riki's eager response diffused his anger. Riki had missed so much in life, he could at least give her this one small experience—never to be repeated, of course—but tonight was special, after all.

Nico nodded slightly and cupped his hands around Riki's head as she sucked him deep.

Riki could hardly believe it when Nico asked Drake to use the dildo on her but she was downright shocked when Drake used his tongue as well. She caught a little of the interplay between the men and heard the soft growl in Nico's throat, hastily bitten back. She liked that he was possessive and liked even more that he'd let this incredible pleasure continue.

She'd never felt so decadent or so wanton. Watching Drake shaft in and out of Estella had been exciting, but to have him do the same to her—albeit with a glass rod instead of his cock—was even more thrilling.

The real thrill of it was in Nico's reaction, oddly enough. Riki found herself watching for his possessive smiles, his pride-filled glances. She felt feminine and beautiful when he looked at her that way, and she'd never felt either of those things before.

Nico's generosity of spirit attracted her as much as his beautiful face, kind eyes and cunning wit. He was her savior and teacher in many respects, but she was fast learning he could be her partner as well. Nico encouraged her to find out who she was and explore her limits. He was perfect for her in every respect. And he was hers.

For the first time in her life, she thought she felt the dragon stirring lazily in her soul, but she couldn't concentrate on that when Drake's tongue began circling her clit. He moved the dildo harder and deeper while his lips closed over the raised nubbin and pulled gently. Riki's hips bucked, but Drake's strong arm held her in place as his mouth closed over her clit and sucked gently.

Riki flew to the stars on a moan. Nico pulled his cock from her mouth as Drake rode her through the powerful orgasm. She looked up to meet her new husband's eyes and read the possessive pride there, as well as the hunger. Nico was still hard and ready.

As Drake held on through the last echoes of pleasure, she felt her response rise again. More. She needed more.

She needed Nico.

"Thanks for warming her up for me." Nico's words were for Drake, but his eyes never left Riki's face.

Drake pulled back, leaving the dildo inside her channel. "It's the least I could do."

"And the most." Nico's gaze moved to his friend with stern warning in his words. The boundary had been drawn, she realized. This was as far as Nico would ever allow him to go. Drake nodded with his ever-present roguish smile and moved off. The message had been delivered and understood.

Drake moved back to Estella, Riki saw out of the corner of her eye. The other woman was recovered now from Drake's earlier pleasuring and apparently ready for more. She welcomed Drake with open legs and he quickly slid into her.

Nico flipped Riki over, handling her as if she were a doll. She liked the sensation, though she would never have tolerated such treatment from anyone but him. Nico positioned her on her hands and knees, bunching a few pillows under her mid-section for added support. The dildo slid out, but he rammed it back in, shocking her a bit.

Nico chuckled at her gasp and slapped her rear for good measure. Riki could feel the moisture between her thighs increasing at the thought of his hands on her and his cock in her. Then she felt the slippery slide of something faintly cold, but warming as Nico stroked it between her cheeks, around the hole there and just slightly within.

"Nico?"

"Ssh, love. It's all right. Tell me if you don't want this but at least give me a chance to prepare you a bit and try. I think you'll enjoy it."

Nico pressed close, his muscular thigh preventing the dildo from sliding out of her pussy. Every now and then he pulsed his leg so the shaft pushed in and then out again as he moved back, fucking her gently, reminding her of its presence. Riki looked sideways, noting the little tub of ointment Nico had open on the table. It was one more of the many things in the decadent tent she either hadn't noticed or understood until now.

The ointment smelled of herbs and she could feel it sliding, with Nico's finger, in and out of her ass, evoking some incredible feelings. Her inner muscles clenched on the glass rod still impaling her as Nico added a second, then a third finger to her ass, stretching her.

Riki moaned when he removed his fingers and moved his cock to her back entrance.

"Push out a little, love. Let me in."

"Nico!" She whimpered, not in protest, but in excitement as he pushed in.

Riki was glad of the pillows he'd stacked beneath her as her arms trembled and gave out. Nico was fully inside her now, moving slowly, as if checking the fit.

"All right?"

Riki sobbed as he began to move gently in and out. "Give it to me harder, Nico. Faster!" she begged.

Nico did move then, giving her what she wanted. He plunged in and out, gentle at first, then harder and longer as she begged him with every motion of her writhing body, every cry from her lips. She was so close, all it took was a few hard plunges into her surprisingly sensitive body and she came, crying out his name in a strangled voice.

Riki heard her name on his lips a moment later as he joined her in pleasure.

ꙮ

The next morning dawned bright and clear. Estella and Drake were gone from the tent when Riki woke, but Nico was there with breakfast and a brilliant smile. They ate together, made love, and then he took her outside the encampment to a small clearing where they could be alone and enjoy the crisp morning.

"I'm glad to see I wasn't too rough on you last night. Or this morning." Nico leaned in to kiss her softly. "How do you feel?"

Riki smiled up at him. "I feel like I could do anything!"

"Anything?" Nico challenged her.

She nodded, willing to see what he might suggest.

"How about flying?"

Riki knew he didn't mean flying as a passenger on his back. He was challenging her to shift. The thought drove fear into her heart, but desire was there too—desire to spread her own wings and take to the sky. It was a fire in her veins as the sleeping dragon within her awakened to her new mate's challenge.

Riki held his gaze as she screwed up her courage and sought the dragon within as never before, willing it to come forward. She actually felt the dragon blink awake, regarding her from within her own soul with startlement for a moment before answering the call. Riki moved aside, letting the dragon form in her mind and in the physical world. She felt the dragon's fire envelop her body as a swirling black mist rose before her eyes.

It was happening!

From one eyeblink to the next, the way she viewed the world changed. Nico now stood below her, refracted in her vision by newly faceted eyes. Her head felt odd, moving sluggishly until she realized her neck was now several feet long. She was a dragon!

I did it! She crowed as Nico shifted before her new eyes. Within moments, he faced her as a dragon, walking right up to her and twining her neck with his own in happiness.

I knew almost from the first, you were meant for me, Riki. After this, you can have no doubt. You are truly my mate in every possible way.

Chapter Thirteen

Far away in the capital of Draconia, Riki's lost family was sitting down to breakfast in the castle.

"The Jinn have taken over the town. It's like a festival down there. You should go see." Prince Collin entered the family dining room as his eldest brother, Roland, rose and went to the long window overlooking the town. His new queen, Lana, sat at the table.

"When did this happen?" Roland asked as he surveyed the town of Castleton, far below. The castle was built into the side of a mountain standing far above the town, sheltering it in its shadow and warmth.

"Overnight, it seems."

A herald came to the door and drew inside, seeking the king's attention.

"Your Majesty, an ambassador from the Jinn has arrived and seeks an immediate audience."

It was unusual, but not unheard of, to entertain ambassadors at breakfast. Roland looked around the room. It was just family here. They all knew of the troubles facing their land and were united in helping him protect the people and dragons of Draconia.

"Show him in."

The herald coughed politely. “It is a woman, Your Majesty. Magda of the Black Dragon Clan is the name she gave.”

Now this was different. Most often, Jinn women were seen and not heard. All Roland’s previous contact had been through male ambassadors, but he was by no means averse to dealing with women.

“Thank you. Show the lady in.”

The herald retreated, appearing a few minutes later with a woman in tow, though she towered over the teen. She was raven-haired and buxom, a fact he saw his younger brothers note with interest. He sent them a private warning.

Put your tongues back in your mouths, boys. This is a diplomat and we cannot afford to offend her.

Lana heard the comment in her mind as well. She rose to greet the woman with a warm smile hiding her amusement.

“Be welcome, Lady Magda. Will you have some breakfast with us?” Lana was already making motions for another place to be set at the long table, across from her and Roland.

The Jinn woman smiled and her beauty only seemed to increase. She had startling green eyes, Roland saw...the color so very familiar.

“You must be Queen Alania. I am Second Steward of the Black Dragon Clan, come to bring news of your sister, Arikia.”

“My sister?” Lana’s face lit with eagerness and went pale with fear at the same time. “What can you tell me of my sister?”

The woman sat as Lana did. Roland took his wife’s hand and squeezed it in support as the other woman spoke.

“Prince Nicolas has found and rescued your sister. They are even now with my people at the Jinnfaire near the northern border of Skithdron. A messenger arrived in the night with the news and bid me gather all the Jinn here, for their homecoming. They were married last night, in the ways of our people, and your sister was crowned Queen of the Jinn."

"What?" Lana's eyes were bright with unshed tears of joy. "Nico and Riki? That's fantastic! But how can she be Queen of the Jinn? Was she with your people all this time?"

Magda shook her head and told them all she knew of Riki's imprisonment and escape. Magda had a great deal of information from reports of the Jinn musicians Lucan employed. They'd watched the sad, green-eyed girl and reported back news of her over the months of her captivity, each separate report coalescing over time to indicate she might be the girl of whom the seers spoke.

Roland listened with quiet interest. What this Jinn woman told them was nothing short of miraculous. When she explained the origins of the Jinn, he was completely astounded to find there were other descendants of Draneth the Wise spread all throughout the lands. Even more fascinating was the idea the Jinn were a matriarchy, not a patriarchy as he had always assumed. Oh, these people were clever. Not even his infamous Spymaster brother had divined all their secrets.

"There is more, Your Majesties," the woman continued speaking as breakfast was all but forgotten. "The Black Dragon Clan counts many shapeshifters among its ranks. I am one. The First Steward, Estella, is another. But we add another to our ranks today. The visions proclaim Queen Arikia of the Jinn will find her wings this very morn. Your brother and his mate will fly home together. They will bring an honor guard of black dragons, sent here as liaisons between our forces and yours."

"More of the Jinn are coming here?" Collin asked from his seat a few feet down the table. "I thought all of them were already in town."

"All who were within a night's ride, Prince Collin," the woman said softly. "The Jinn are numerous and spread all over the lands in many different clans, but all are ruled by my sister, Estella, Steward of the Black Dragon Clan and now, by your sister, our new Queen, as well. Our seers tell us a time is coming soon when our forces will unite and fight together to prevent catastrophe for all the lands."

Roland stood, pacing, while he tried to absorb the strange turn of events.

"Your news is both welcome and troubling," he said at length. "While I'm overjoyed my wife's sister has been found and my brother married," he could still hardly believe that part of it, "I'm concerned by these dark visions of the future. While I respect the reputation and skill of your Jinn seers, I can only hope they're wrong about what's coming." He held up one hand to forestall the argument he could see forming on the woman's lips. "Nevertheless, all help is welcome, and new black dragon kin even more so. I'm pleased to welcome your people as allies, Magda, and hope we can find a way to work well together."

The raven-haired girl beamed at him then, and he saw his brothers' jaws drop as her beauty stunned them. Luckily, the Jinn magic had no effect on him. He loved Lana too much to have his head turned by a pretty girl. Jinn or no.

"With your permission then," Magda rose and ruffled her full skirts around her legs, "we will set an encampment to the east of the existing town, at the base of the castle mount, bordered by the river tributary on the east, the existing town on the west and the open fields to the south."

"You planned ahead, I see," Roland teased as she grinned. "Just how many of your brethren are you expecting?"

Magda shrugged daintily. "Several thousand at least, by week's end. Castletown will become a city by month's end, and we have plans to develop the open fields to the east, to grow crops to support our people. If we have your permission, of course."

Roland knew when he'd been outfoxed. The Jinn were making plans to settle in Draconia. The idea was mind boggling. The Jinn, who were known far and wide as homeless nomads, were putting down roots in Draconia. At the base of his castle, no less. Never did he think he'd see anything like this in his time.

"Your people are welcome to farm any land not already claimed, Magda, but you realize we must keep the herds for our dragon kin, right?"

Magda laughed and the tinkling sound had his younger brothers squirming in their seats. "But of course! The Black Dragon Clan, above all, knows the importance of working with dragons. We have no desire to rule, but we will fly into battle at your direction, King Roland. We will need training though, with your Lairs. Unfortunately, flying is something we have only done in secret up 'til now and we need more practice working with other dragons in battle."

Just at that moment, a dragon-sized door opened at the end of the large family chamber and a gleaming silver dragonet tumbled in. He was huge by dragonet standards and far shinier than any other dragon in the land, but he was family. Tor, the baby Ice Dragon, stopped short when he saw a visitor in the room, eyeing her carefully as he came to sit on his haunches behind Lana and Roland.

"Son, this is Second Steward Magda of the Black Dragon Clan of the Jinn. Her people will be building on to the town below."

Greetings, Sir Tor. Magda surprised them all by speaking in the silent way of dragons. *I've heard much about you.*

Lana, they all heard Tor's words in their minds, *she feels like a dragon. Like you and Roland.*

Magda laughed, the pleasant sound teasing everyone's senses. *That's because I am.*

ཌྀ

Riki spread her wings, flying in a secluded area near the Jinn encampment with Nico watching over her every move, coaching and coaxing in the most loving way. The feeling was just amazing. She'd never felt so free in her life, or so happy. The man she loved flew beside her, guiding her, showing her how to be a dragon, encouraging her and yet, letting her fly free. He was such a special, thoughtful, attentive partner, but never stifling. He was just perfect.

A slithering form below caught her eye and struck fear into Riki's heart.

Skiths. A lot of them. Heading straight for the Jinn encampment.

Nico!

I see them. His voice sounded grimly through Riki's mind. *Come on, we've got to warn the Jinn.*

Turning more sharply than Riki could follow, Nico winged back toward the Jinn encampment, but she wasn't quite so agile in the sky yet. Cutting her corner too tightly, Riki began to lose altitude, coming dangerously close to the skiths far below.

Nico!

But it was too late. Riki's panic translated poorly in her newfound dragon body. She began to tumble, falling closer and closer to the danger below. In her panic, she began to shift, the black mist swirling as her body instinctively sought a more familiar form. The wings slowed her descent at first, bringing her closer to the canopy of tall trees, but then the wings were gone and she started to pick up speed.

Riki reached out blindly, falling through the tops of the trees, breaking the smaller branches near the tops, slowing her descent once again. Leaves and branches struck her tumbling body, slapping her in the face and causing her to cry out in pain until finally she came to rest with a jolting thud.

Caught in a tree.

Blessed be the Mother of All.

Riki! The black dragon trumpeted Nico's distress as he made his way back to where she'd fallen.

I'm all right. I landed in a tree. I'm pretty high up. I don't think the skiths can reach me up here.

But they certainly had spotted her. Nico could see that easily enough from his position above. Several of the deadly creatures paused at the base of her tree, trying experimentally to spit at her, but thankfully, she really was out of their range.

Can you shift and fly out? Nico knew it was a long shot. She was too new to her wings to be able to shift and fly from such an awkward position.

I doubt it. Not right now, anyway. I'm too shaken up. I'm content just to stay here for a bit. Nico, you have to go warn the Jinn.

I can't leave you!

You must. Nico, even the magical circle around the encampment won't keep out this many skiths. This is an attack. An organized one. Even I know this many skiths don't just appear on their own. Especially not this far north.

Nico had to acknowledge she was right. Someone had herded these skiths to attack the Jinnfaire. The people on the ground were mostly defenseless against such fierce creatures. Only dragons could adequately defend against an army of skiths, with their fire. It was the one thing skiths were afraid of.

But the Jinn claimed there were black dragons among them. Perhaps there would be enough to defend the huge number of people at the Jinnfaire. He wasn't sure, but it really was their only shot.

Nico, you have to help them!

I don't want to leave you.

But you have to. You must.

Nico sighed with resignation. He knew what he had to do.

You're right. Nico flew in a circle above Riki for a moment more, wishing he could kiss her, knowing he couldn't. *Stay right there, sweetheart. Don't move a muscle. You should be safe from the skiths where you are, so don't try to go anywhere else, all right?*

Believe me, I won't move an inch. I'm still shaking too badly, for one thing. Her little chuckle carried through her thoughts. Sweet Mother! How he loved this woman.

All right. I'll be back as soon as possible, with help. Stay right where you are and remember that I love you more than anything in this world. His thoughts softened as he turned to wing away toward the Jinn encampment. *Without you, I'm lost, Riki. Stay safe for me, my dearest love.*

I love you too, Nico. Warn the people, then hurry back to me.

Riki sat in the tree, content to be safe for the moment from the spitting skiths so far below. Most had given up on her, but a few still lingered at the base of her tree, keeping her penned.

The rest were moving steadily toward the Jinn encampment and that worried her. Those people had little to defend themselves against such a massive incursion of the deadly creatures.

But they claimed to have a few dragons among their number. She'd seen one already when Estella changed right in front of her. So they had some protection, at least. They would probably need Riki's healing skills when it was over though. People and dragons were sure to be injured and she would do all she could to help heal them. They'd been so kind to her, she wanted to help them in return.

Is that you, little witch?

A sickening, slithering voice sounded through her mind in a perversion of the way she communicated with Nico. Riki looked around for the source of the voice. Someone was watching her. Fear skittered through her already adrenaline-charged body.

Come, little witch. She would swear it was Lucan's voice. *Come home to me, little witch, or my brothers will sever your head and eat your entrails.*

She felt the anger rising with the words, but where were they coming from? Lucan was nowhere to be seen. In fact, she couldn't see one single human within range of her high perch. The only living things left in the area were skiths. All the animals had fled before the evil creatures or been eaten.

Then Riki noticed one skith in particular seemed to be watching her. The others slithered around below the tree in a mass of scaly flesh, but this one stood apart, its slitted eyes trained on her. It made her skin crawl.

This was where the voice originated. Could Lucan somehow channel his thoughts through the skiths? The idea was terrifying, but it explained why these skiths were so far north and why they were heading en masse toward the Jinn encampment without a single human soldier driving them.

Lucan was controlling the skiths.

It was the only explanation.

Loralie had warned of this, in her oblique way, all those months ago. She'd told Lucan, in Riki's presence, how he might discover a way to communicate with and control the creatures with which he was blending his essence. Lucan had crowed in delight at the thought, but Riki had always felt the significant look Loralie gave her was meant as a sort of warning. She hadn't understood it at the time, but many things she'd seen and heard back then, were starting to make a horrific sort of sense.

Lucan could not only control the skiths, but he could see through their eyes. And he'd found her. He knew exactly where she was. Panic set in until she realized she was well and truly stuck in this tree. To move was suicide. To stay was even worse. Lucan would send his men to recapture her and who knows what tortures he would think up when he finally had her back in his control.

Despair washed over her. The only choice she had left was how she would die. Should she wait to be recaptured and let Lucan kill her by slow degrees over the course of what could easily be years? Or should she jump and end it quick, letting a skith sever her head?

Anger rose up to smother the fear Lucan struck in her soul. There was another choice.

Defiance.

And this time she wasn't alone. Nico would help her. He would return for her any moment, and the Jinn had promised their aid as well. She could do this. She could stand up to Lucan for the first time in her life, and she knew there would be others standing with her, if she needed them. She wasn't alone anymore.

"Damn you!" she screamed at the evil creature. "Damn you to the seven hells and back again!"

Anger bubbled up and with it came the heat and fire of the dragon. Never before had it been so close to the surface, though she recognized it as the power that had lain dormant in her soul all her life. Only now, she could tap into it.

Riki reveled in the fire, letting the power bathe her soul in its purity. Renewed, she opened her eyes and pointed to the skith.

Flames shot from her outstretched hand, shocking her. But it felt right. The flame was real enough, but it did not burn her, for it was *of* her, part of her very soul.

Calling on the fire of her dragon nature, Riki poured all she had into the flame, sending it to the skith through which Lucan watched, reveling in its screams of death.

The other skiths scattered, slithering away from the flame that burned pure and hot. This was magical flame and it consumed only the skith, leaving the forest around it unburned.

Riki felt triumph rage through her. She'd just killed a creature that should never have lived in the first place. For some reason, that knowledge made her feel good, though she'd never taken a life before. Riki had been taught as a child that all life was sacred, but she'd learned the hard way some things were too evil to live.

Lucan was one of those. Skiths were another.

Killing the skith didn't fill her with the dread she expected. Instead, she felt...not exactly happy...but rather, justified. She felt the rightness of her actions and would shed no tears over it.

Skiths were just...wrong. She felt it in her soul. They didn't belong to this world and should never have been created.

That was it. That's the secret knowledge that clicked into place, though she had no idea how she knew it. Skiths were no creatures of nature. No, they'd been created by wizards, and evil wizards at that.

Riki didn't know where the knowledge came from, but she didn't question it. Nico might know the truth. She would ask him when he returned.

Nico arrived at the encampment in the nick of time to warn the Jinn about the oncoming army of skiths. He was amazed by the way these nomadic people responded to his trumpeting cry. Within moments, a legion of black dragons flew over the sprawling encampment. Nico had never seen the like. At least a dozen black dragons filled the sky.

When Draconian forces took to the sky, the dragons came in a rainbow of colors, with leather-clad knights on their backs. Once in a while, a black dragon would lead such a contingent, but there were precious few blacks left in his homeland. This, though, was an embarrassment of riches. Nothing but riderless black dragons filled the air over the camp while the Jinn scurried in organized chaos below.

Wagons moved to encircle the tents and barricades of all kinds sprang up around the perimeter. Men with sharp weapons stood ready behind the barricades and rows of women stood ready behind them, armed with longbows. Other women—the old and the very young—stood ready with braziers and oil to light the arrows and do other tasks to help the fighters.

But the dragons were disorganized. Nico could easily see they'd never fought in formation before. They were like young recruits, not knowing how to keep out of each other's way.

There was little time to organize them and no time for diplomacy. Nico flew into their midst and took charge, dividing them into pairs and assigning sectors like the general of dragons and men he truly was. None questioned his right to command them, and within short order, the defense was ready.

Just in time, too, for the skiths encircled the camp and attacked from all directions at once. Nico had just enough time to offer up a prayer to the Mother of All before diving into the fray, flaming skiths as he went, with the help of the other black dragons.

Where is your mate? Estella flew close, frying skiths with broad swaths of her flame as she passed.

She's safe for now. Look out behind you!

Damn these creatures! Anger filled the woman's words, along with frustration as a stream of venom narrowly missed her. *How do your knights and dragons do this day in and day out?*

It is a lifelong quest, Nico answered soberly, keeping an eye on the entire battlefield. He had to shore the Jinn dragons up, darting in where needed. Already three of the Jinn dragons were badly hurt and out of the fighting. Women on the ground were dousing their venom wounds with water and healers were tending them.

This is a battle for which we are ill prepared. I see that clearly now, Estella's determination sounded through his mind as she flew past. *But that will change. Prince Nicolas, you must see to Riki. Her safety is crucial.*

Nico looked around at the battle. The Jinn dragons were sloppy fighters in the air, but they were getting the job done. Over half of the massed skiths were dead already and the rest would soon be joining them, a result of both the skilled assault of the ground fighters and the disjointed dragons fighting from the air. He judged they were well on their way to victory, which meant he was free to go rescue his new wife from that tree.

He'd just turned in the direction of her perch when a single black dragon flew over the forest.

Riki!

Sorry I'm late. Humor and love sounded through her voice in his mind. The other dragons welcomed her with trumpeting cries and she answered in return, though her voice was unsteady—so unused to being a dragon she was.

By the Mother, am I glad to see you.

Me too, Nico. Me too. Relief sounded through her voice and he was never happier to hear her wry spark of humor. *Uh, Nico? Um...how do I get down?*

He chuckled and smoke issued from his dragon mouth. *Watch me first. I'll set down on the ground and catch you. All right?*

I'll try.

Joy filled him, just watching his remarkable mate. Landing skillfully in the center of the encampment, he picked a clear area so she'd have a little room to maneuver. Nico turned, holding out his wings, coaching his mate into his arms.

Aim for me, sweetheart. This is the way we teach our babies. Maybe someday soon, we'll have a baby of our own to teach, eh? He couldn't resist teasing and chuckled when her wing beats faltered at the idea.

Really? A baby?

She seemed astounded at the idea. *Yes, my love, our baby. A little prince or princess to love and cherish. Part of us. Part of our love. Didn't you think of that when you agreed to be mine?*

I hadn't gotten that far yet. She chuckled and he saw smoke streaming out behind her as she aimed her flight path for him. *I don't want to hurt you. Just let me tumble if I land hard, all right?*

Sweetheart, you could never hurt me. Trust me to catch you and protect you. It's what I was born to do.

You say the sweetest things. Her voice sounded softly through his mind. *Watch out now, here I come.*

You're doing fine.

Nico continued to encourage her as she slowed and dropped, aiming for him. She stumbled a bit at first, but all in all, she made a good showing for her very first landing. Nico caught her in his strong dragon arms, twining his neck with hers in a dragonish hug. She was so beautiful, so brave and special. She fit him in every possible way.

Riki stepped back, facing Nico as she willed the shift. When she stood once more in human form, she was fully dressed, but her feet were bare. She peered down at her toes in puzzlement as Nico chuckled smoke.

"Where are my shoes?"

Elsewhere, obviously. Sweetheart, when you shift, you have to hold the image of your clothing—all of your clothing—to you when you come back. Actually, you should be quite proud. Most first-timers come back completely naked. You have your dress at least.

"And my wedding band." She held up the glittering gold ring to show him and it sparkled in the sun. Nico growled and it sounded like pure male satisfaction to her. "But I really liked those boots. How can I get them back?"

Want to try again? Shift to dragon, then back again. Picture yourself fully clothed, including your pretty boots.

She did so, noting that each time she shifted, it became easier. When she stood before Nico once more in human form, her boots were on her feet and a wide smile adorned her face.

You're a natural.

They both turned as a dragon trumpeted in distress.

"You'd better go help them. I'll help the healers."

Stay in the center of the camp. Promise me you won't get out near the edges. The ground fighters are better than the dragons, but some of the skiths still might get through.

"Don't worry, I'll stay safe."

She hugged the secret of her newly discovered ability to throw flame even in human form, close to her heart. She'd tell Nico when they had more time. Right now, those Jinn dragons needed him. It was clear, even to her, they were not very well organized in their flight. Riki had already seen several near misses in the air and was glad to be on the ground, out of the way.

Nico took to the sky with a powerful beat of his wings. No matter how often she saw him in dragon form, he never failed to impress her. He was so beautiful, so competent, so sure of himself and his direction. She wished she could be just half as sure of herself, but she was getting there. With each new discovery, each little success, she was learning just who she was and what she could do.

Soon, she hoped, she would be a woman Nico could be proud of—and that she could be proud of herself. Little by little, she worked toward that goal.

Looking around at the scurrying Jinn, Riki set off in the direction of the injured dragons. She knew what to do for skith venom wounds all too well and would be happy to help these brave people.

Chapter Fourteen

About an hour later, the last skith was dead.

The Jinn dragons were rolling around in a stream not far away, washing the droplets of venom off their black hides before returning to camp. Riki helped the wounded alongside a surprisingly large contingent of highly skilled Jinn healers. They even taught her a little about how to use her power without draining herself too badly. They were good people, who showed her both respect and kindness, bolstering her self-esteem in the process.

Riki? Nico's voice sounded through her mind. *Where are you?*

I'm in the big yellow tent. They've gathered all the wounded here.

Can you get away or do they need you?

Riki surveyed the orderly room. There were far more skilled healers than herself here and they had things well under control.

I'll come. Where are you?

At Estella's tent. There's a war council of sorts gathering.

Good. I have something to tell them.

Really? Curiosity sounded in his words and she smiled.

Yes, really.

What is it?

Wait and see. She couldn't resist teasing him. *I'll be right there.*

Nico was waiting for her in front of the tent. He pulled her into his arms the moment he saw her. Nico kissed her deeply, his relief communicating itself through the kiss as he molded her to his strong body.

"I love you," he said as he drew back, looking down into her eyes.

No matter how many times she heard him say the words, they always had the same effect on her. Wonder and joy shone through her spirit. Nico loved her!

Nothing could rival the feeling of knowing his love.

Nico kissed her again before she could respond, and then stepped back slightly, motioning for her to enter the tent before him. What she found inside was a grim group of faces, dusty and dirty from the hours just spent defending their very lives.

Riki felt a great sense of responsibility for these people. She'd brought Lucan's wrath down on them.

Silently she walked to the table and stood before them. Conversation ceased as all eyes turned to her. Her mouth went dry, but she knew she had to speak.

"I apologize." She paused, gathering her courage. "I brought the skiths here. Lucan was looking for me and attacked you because of it. I am deeply sorry."

Stunned silence met her words until Estella spoke.

"How can you be so sure this was your fault? We don't blame you."

"Well, then you should. I know because Lucan spoke to me through one of the skiths." Shocked gasps met her statement.

"He directs them with his mind. He has power over them now, since he merged with them."

"Merged?" Arabetta's voice was grave with worry.

"Lucan is no longer human." Grave silence met Nico's announcement. "At least not completely. He's part skith now. I saw it myself. He talks to them." Nico stepped up behind Riki, standing close with her back against his chest, offering his support.

"And he talks through them," Riki confirmed. "He sees through their eyes and was able to communicate with me through one of them."

"What did he say?"

Riki shrugged. "He wanted me back. Or dead. No surprise there. I was the only thing keeping him alive and out of pain. Without me around to heal him constantly, he'll be in agony."

"So he'll be looking for another healer," Arabetta said shrewdly. "We must get the word out." Nods all around the table confirmed the grave need to warn other healers. Riki hadn't even thought of that, but it was an excellent idea. Still...

"Loralie told him he needed a special healer and that I was the only one in Skithdron."

"A dragon healer then," Estella said without doubt, but Riki was shocked by her assumption.

"I'm not—"

Nico stopped her words with a quick squeeze of his arm around her middle.

Oh, yes you are a dragon healer. Never doubt that, my love. It is a gift of your heritage. Female descendants of Draneth the Wise are usually able to heal dragons.

I had no idea.

And until this morning, you'd never shifted either, so don't doubt it. You have much within you that you're only just discovering. Personally, I'm going to love every minute of learning just who and what you are.

Nico's warm arm around her waist branded her, firing her blood, as did the sexy tone of his voice in her mind.

"What happened to the skith Lucan was using?" Estella's question shocked Riki back to the conversation.

"I killed it."

Silence met her words until Nico asked simply, "How?"

She turned in his arms and it was as if only the two of them existed. "At first I was so scared. I'm embarrassed to admit I considered jumping out of the tree to let the skiths have at me. At least they would give me a quick end, or so I thought. But then I thought of you," she reached up to cup his cheeks in her hands, "and I got angry."

Nico chuckled. "Thinking of me made you angry?"

"No." She smiled at his teasing. "Thinking of Lucan threatening you—and me—made me angry. The fire bubbled up and before I knew it, flame came from my hand and fried the skith."

"Sweet Mother!" someone at the table gasped, reminding Riki they had an audience.

Arabetta stood, her smile kind. "Can you show us, child? Can you," she looked around the tent, her old eyes lighting on the cold central fire pit, "direct your flame over there, for example?"

Riki tilted her head, thinking. "I don't know, but I'll try if you like." She stepped out of Nico's arms and clear of the table, summoning the fire within her blood and trying to aim for the shallow pit filled with stones. The blue flame came forth, crackling against the stones, but not setting fire to any of the twigs that had been set for kindling. "It did that in the forest too. It burned the skith, but not the grass or dead wood."

Riki stopped and turned back to the table, surprised by the nearly uniform looks of awe directed at her. Only Nico smiled, grinning from ear to ear as he watched her.

"It is as it was foretold," Arabetta spoke at last, breaking the silence. "Her magic burns evil alone."

The gathered Jinn whispered excitedly among themselves while Arabetta and Estella watched her with new respect in their eyes.

"I don't understand. I mean, I know this is a strange development. I was shocked by it, but why are you so amazed. I thought the Jinn were comfortable with magic of all kinds."

"Magic, yes," Arabetta nodded. "It is part of our daily lives. But this kind of magic is something special, even for us. This magic could be our salvation in the fight to come."

"Speaking of which..." Nico drew their attention away from her, thankfully. She had a lot to think about and was still uncomfortable being the center of attention. "If Lucan sees through the skiths' eyes, he surely knows what's happened and where we are. He'll be sending soldiers to finish the job."

Grave nods met his assessment. "We must disperse," Estella said strongly and all nodded in agreement, "but before we do, we must arrange for your escape across the northern border and then into Draconia. We've also learned this day how badly prepared we are to fight as dragons. That has got to change. I've already sent a messenger to our people in Draconia. They will be meeting with your brother to bring him up to date on your travels and also to request training for our dragons in your Lairs."

Nico nodded, a smile on his face. “Roland will be surprised, but all dragons are welcome in Draconia. Black dragons especially so.”

“Good.” Estella smiled as well. “Then you’ll enjoy the company of five of our kind on your journey home. They will act as honor guard, decoys, and emissaries to your land. You’ll leave tonight, as will all the Jinn. This Jinnfaire must be concluded with all possible haste and our people dispersed to avoid Lucan’s soldiers. It’s no longer safe for Jinn in Skithdron.” She addressed the leaders sitting around the big tent. “Spread the word to all the Brotherhood.”

Nico and Riki were among the last to leave, their parting with Drake bittersweet.

“Won’t you come home with us?” Nico asked his old friend, already knowing the answer.

“Not yet. Besides, you’ll make much better time without me along, and I can’t leave my instruments and my wagon.”

Riki stepped close to hug Drake, though Nico had to hold back his growls as Drake held her a little too tightly. “Thank you for all you’ve done.” She kissed his cheek.

Drake swooped in and kissed her lips, laughing when Nico tugged Riki out of his arms, effectively ending the kiss. Drake winked at her flushed face and she giggled like a carefree girl. The sound lightened Nico’s heart, and he forgave Drake’s outrageous behavior.

“We’ll all meet again. I promise you.” Drake shook the hand Nico offered, then surprised him by dropping to one knee. “Nicolas, I swore to serve you years ago as Prince and Spymaster to the King of Draconia. I renew my vow now to you as King-Consort of the Jinn Brotherhood. If ever you need me, just call. Any service I can perform, for you or your queen, I will do gladly."

Nico felt the gravity of Drake's vow, and the slight tingle of magic shooting from where their hands were still joined. He didn't question the new title yet, though his thoughts were racing. Slowly, he placed his other hand on Drake's shoulder and tugged him to his feet.

"I accept your oath, Drake, and welcome your friendship and service." Formality done, he hugged the other man close, pounding him on the back once for good measure. When he released his old friend, his face was confused. "What's this King-Consort stuff?"

"Didn't you realize? By marrying our Riki here," Drake laughed and winked at Riki, making her smile, "you became, in effect, King and Spymaster of the Jinn? Your network has just increased five-fold, Nico. The eyes of the Brotherhood now report to you."

"And who led them before?" Nico had a sneaking suspicion, but it needed confirmation.

"Why, I did, of course!" Drake laughed, setting Nico's mind at ease. Taking over someone else's network was risky at best, but if the network was Drake's to begin with, the situation just became a whole lot easier to deal with.

"Then you will continue, Drake of the Five Lands—Drake of Draconia—to serve as Spymaster for the Brotherhood of the Jinn." Nico used his best formal voice even though his heart was light with laughter. "But you'll have to let me know what's going on now, of course."

Drake bowed his head, all smiles. "Of course, my liege."

"You sly dog. I've been trying to crack the Brotherhood's spy network for years."

Drake laughed. "Yes, I know."

"And you've been leading me in circles, haven't you? I ought to pummel you for that, my friend."

"You can try," Drake dared him, laughing all the while. "But think of it this way...you've finally got an in with the Brotherhood and it cost you nothing at all."

Drake walked away then, leaving them with a smile and a wave as he jumped aboard his loaded wagon and drove out. He was whistling as he left them, waving as they waved back.

"He's wrong, you know." Nico pulled Riki into his arms as they watched Drake drive off. "It cost me my heart. But that's a price I'm more than willing to pay."

ജ്ദ

For someone who had only just discovered they could become a dragon that morning, Riki flew beautifully that evening as they took off with their five new black dragon friends for the north. Nico marveled at how quickly the Jinn had dispersed. One moment a giant gathering had filled the encampment, the next all that was left was a circle of smoldering skith corpses. Nothing of the Jinn remained. Even the grass cooperated, looking as if nothing had trod upon it in ages. The land was as pristine as it had been before the Jinn arrived. Only the dead skiths marred the beautiful, forest landscape.

Their honor guard flew in formation, one in front, one on either side of Nico and Riki, and two behind, guarding their backs. They hadn't known at first what positions to take until Nico gently guided them into a formation used regularly in Draconia.

Of the five black dragons, two were female and three male. Of the females, one was about Riki's age, or perhaps a few years older. Her name was Kira and she flew to Riki's side, quite obviously hoping to make friends with someone near her own age. She looked to be a fierce fighter as well. When she'd walked up, decked out in leather from head to toe just like a male warrior, Nico had taken a second look. Jinn women were known for their bright dresses and gold jewelry, but this girl was very different.

The other female was older and had a more mystical quality about her. Although she looked like she could handle herself in a fight, she had healer written all over her and Estella had confirmed she was, in fact, a seer as well. Zallra was her name and she had asked to come on the trip because of a vision she shared with none but Arabetta.

The men were all seasoned fighters, though Arabetta had confided to Nico that one of them, an older man named Seth, had quite a bit of magic at his disposal. The other two were twins named Jase and Jeffry. They fought as a unit both on the ground and in the sky. They, of all the black dragons, were the most likely to be able to fight well from the air, under Nico's command, without much training. Nico was glad to have them and as they winged their way through the dark night over the northern border of Skithdron, Nico was glad to talk with them all and make friends.

Because all the skiths in the area had been herded to attack the Jinn, they crossed into the Northlands with relative ease. Only a few soldiers' watchtowers had to be skirted or otherwise avoided, and all in all, Nico was surprised by how easily their escape from Skithdron had been accomplished. Still, they weren't home yet. They had to traverse the cold northlands, heading for Draconia.

Nico decided their best bet was to make for the Northern Lair. It hadn't been too long since Salomar's defeat, so the area near the Lair should be relatively free of obstruction. There were those diamond-tipped weapons to be wary of, though. Salomar might be gone, but his armies of brigands survived for the most part. Nico knew it was only a matter of time before a warlord or two rose to replace Salomar.

As night turned slowly toward day, Nico sighted the shining waters of Crystal Lake. They would be able to sleep the day away in a secret cove he knew there. Silently, he signaled to the contingent of dragons, altering their course slightly toward the lake. They followed his lead smoothly, having learned through the long night how to fly in formation as he had them rotate positions every half hour. It was the way he drilled young dragons and knights and it worked well with these black dragons too.

Riki, too, was flying better with each stroke of her wings. They stopped from time to time to rest, but she was keeping up, new as she was to flying. He felt pride in her, though Nico knew his bride was going to be very sore when they finally stopped for the day.

Still, it couldn't be helped. Every step closer to Draconia was a step closer to safety and he had to take them as quickly as possible. Too much was at stake. Riki's safety was paramount, but there were other considerations as well. Nico had learned much on this odyssey about the threat they all faced. Roland needed to know these things and word needed to spread to all possible allies. The safety of all lands was at stake.

What's that? Riki asked in the silence of his mind. She was still getting used to her enhanced dragon vision, and had asked him several times what they were looking at from above as they passed over.

Crystal Lake. We'll stop there for the day to rest.

How close are we to the border with Draconia?

Not far now. Can you see where the rocks give way to trees just on the other side of the lake? The first gray streaks of dawn were on the horizon, lighting it well for dragon sight.

I can see some big brown blurs and some big green blurs but that's about it.

He chuckled, sending a stream of smoke out behind them. *Well, you can trust me on this, the border is not far ahead, on the other side of the lake.*

Then why stop on this side? Don't you want to be in Draconia before we rest?

I'd love that, but it's not possible for several reasons. First, the lake is much wider than it looks from here. It will take hours to traverse and we would be vulnerable to She Who Lives in the Lake should we try to cross it during the hours of daylight.

She Who Lives in the Lake? What's in there? Some kind of monster?

Not a monster, exactly, but it's better to cross under cover of darkness to avoid her notice. Also, the Draconian side of the lake is wild and mostly uninhabited. I wouldn't trust Lucan not to have sent soldiers or skiths—or both—to hary us there. I also know a place on this side, which is well protected enough that we can sleep the day away in relative ease. We'll stop here for the day, fish, eat, wash up and sleep, then cross the lake tonight, under cover of darkness.

And then what? I mean, where are we heading for after that?

Then we make for the Northern Lair. It's not far past the lake. We should be able to land there several hours before dawn. And won't they be surprised to see us? Your sister roused them when she brought a wild northern Ice Dragon home with her, but you're bringing five black dragons. I think you've got her beat. Nico chuckled, sending smoke out behind him, and Riki joined in, coughing a little as she got used to the workings of her dragon throat and the flame always kept banked within.

I don't care if I beat her at anything. I just want to see her!

Nico moved to the left, riding the air currents as he led the rest of the dragons to the place he alone knew. Or so he thought. In the dim morning light, he could just make out a huge silver dragonet splashing around in the shallows...fishing.

Tor, is that you?

Uncle Nico? Came the young voice piping through all the dragons' minds. *Where are you?*

Right above you, boy. We'll be landing any moment. Is Lana with you? And Roland?

Yes. They're sleeping in the tent. They always sleep so much nowadays.

Nico chuckled at Tor's artless words. He realized he'd better give his brother some warning since he was bringing company. Nico was careful to send his thoughts to Roland alone.

Rol! Stop fucking your wife for a minute and come outside. You're not going to believe what I'm bringing you as a present.

The contingent of black dragons touched down as dawn kissed the sky. Six of them landed first, the last one circling behind, waiting her turn and working up her nerve. Riki chose her spot and aimed for the ground, closing her eyes at the last moment as she came in too fast and ended up tumbling ass over tea kettle into the shallow part of the lake.

The shining silver dragonet was the first to come over, his diamond eyes sparkling as he laughed. Riki couldn't hold on to her embarrassment when her antics so clearly amused the young dragon.

Who are you? she asked the big youngster.

I'm Tor. You're funny. You land like Lana.

Lana? Hope rose in Riki's throat as she looked around at the dragons, shifting to human form one by one. And then she noticed the small black tent and the woman stepping from it. *Lana!*

Riki's heart broke open and joy filled her spirit. She stumbled out of the water, shaking off her big dragon body, thinking of her warm, dry clothing as she shifted form quickly to face the woman who was her twin.

"Lana?" she asked tentatively.

"Riki!" The other woman moved closer, then ran forward and pulled Riki into her arms, hugging her close. It was her sister. Her twin. Riki felt the two halves of their souls rejoining as they'd once been when they were children. "Riki!" Lana cried tears of joy, just as Riki did, the twins reunited and hugging each other close for long, long minutes.

She looks just like Lana, they both heard Tor whisper to the others some time later.

It was Lana who turned toward the big silver dragon. "Tor, baby, this is my sister, Riki. I told you about her, remember?" Lana turned to her sister and smiled. "Riki, this is Tor. My best friend and companion these past years. I never would have made it without him."

Riki greeted the young dragon, amazed by the sparkling sight of him. He was gorgeous...and just a baby, though he was huge.

You fly just like Lana did in the beginning. I can show you how to land better if you want.

His youthful eagerness touched her heart and she smiled at him, but Nico came up behind her, in human form now, and caught her around the waist. He laughed up at Tor, apparently well familiar with the young dragon.

"Have pity on her, Tor. She only learned how to fly yesterday."

"Yesterday?" A new male voice entered the conversation and Riki looked up at the tall man holding her sister's hand. He looked a lot like Nico, but his eyes were emerald green.

"I didn't know I could shift until yesterday." Riki looked at the happiness in her sister's eyes as she snuggled up to the tall man. "You must be Roland."

He nodded, pulling Lana back against him much the way Nico held her. "And you're Arikia. Welcome home."

Riki's heart was so full, her eyes welled with tears, but she refused to let them fall. She was too happy to mar the moment with tears.

"Roland is my husband," Lana clarified.

"Yes, I heard. Congratulations to you both." Riki answered, thankful for Nico's warm body at her back. "I married Nico the day before yesterday."

Lana's smile was wide and genuine. "Yes, I heard that too. Congratulations to you both, but, Riki, are you sure you know what you're getting into? The Prince of Spies is more than a handful, from all accounts."

The teasing question made her laugh. "Oh, I wouldn't have it any other way."

Epilogue

As it turned out, a small contingent of Jinn were on hand just inside the circle of trees to greet their brethren. Magda had insisted on accompanying Roland and Lana to meet with Nico and Riki. Roland brought his own men with him as well, so there were a couple of dragons and knights along with the Jinn, guarding their king and queen from a respectful distance.

They made camp for the day, the soldiers among them guarding while the family caught up with all the news. Roland was troubled by Nico and Riki's accounts of Lucan's transformation and his ability to direct the skiths. He was also astounded by the idea that his younger brother was not only married, but also now King-Consort of the Jinn Brotherhood.

They crossed the lake after dark and arrived in the Northern Lair a few hours before dawn. As expected the arrival of so many black dragons raised eyebrows all over the Lair. The dragons of the Lair saw the blacks' arrival as a sign of great hope, trumpeting their joy to the sky and setting up quite a stir.

Roland was glad to leave the arrangements for housing all the visitors to Sir Hal, Sir Jures and the Lady Candis, leaders of the Northern Lair while he sought a bedchamber for himself and Lana. But a surprise awaited him when Hal found a moment of privacy. The knight handed Roland a letter, his eyes grave.

"This came from the witch Loralie, for you, my liege. It arrived last night, though how she knew you'd be here today, I have no idea."

Roland accepted the letter, his eyes narrowed. "She *is* a witch, after all."

"I'll be standing by if you need me, sire." Hal nodded once and moved off.

Roland stole a moment away from his family to read the letter. He didn't want to ruin their arrival home with this just yet. First he would read it and see what the letter contained. Only then would he decide what was to be done. Still he knew, coming from Loralie, it couldn't be good news.

Roland sat on the edge of Tilden and Rue's wallow. The elder dragons of the Northern Lair, they were highly ranked and sat on the Dragon Council. Roland had known and respected them both all his life. They watched, silently supporting him as he read the letter.

The contents of it weighed heavy on his mind, but he didn't want to ruin Lana's reunion with her twin just yet. First, he had to sort through what Loralie's letter might truly mean. He didn't trust the North Witch. Not at all.

Have you ever heard of the Wizard Skir? Roland asked the dragons.

Tilden reared back and smoke issued from his throat to drift toward the vents in the ceiling. Roland could clearly see his agitation.

That name is not spoken among dragonkind, sire. He is cursed for all time for his evil. Rue spoke calmly, but her voice was adamant in Roland's mind.

Loralie claims he is imprisoned in a place called the Citadel and it is this place Lucan means to go, to free him.

Both dragons reared back at this news, clearly upset. *This cannot be allowed!* Tilden thundered, anger and fear mixed in his tone along with grim determination.

Roland watched the dragons' reactions carefully, weighing their response against Loralie's words and whatever she wished to accomplish by her missive. He didn't trust her, but the true fear he witnessed in two of the oldest and most respected dragons in his land was not to be discounted.

Why? What did Skir do to earn eternal imprisonment from his peers? Few of the wizards had any high moral standards if the old tales are to be believed. Why single out this one to lock away forever in ice?

Cold silence met his question until finally Rue stepped forward, her jeweled eyes grim, her voice in Roland's mind laced with seething anger and incomprehensible distress.

The Wizard Skir is the one who created the skiths. To destroy all dragons.

The Siren

Off in the dark, of a cold lonely sea
She cries at night for her loves yet to be
The Siren, she wails, and her song splits the sky
A young man is entranced on the ship passing by

...I am the Siren and this is my song...

Tossing care to the waves, he then steps o'er the side
A smile lights his face and a tear sparks her eye
He reaches to her, his arms open wide
But he grasps only moonbeams that dance on the tide

...I am the Siren and this is my song...

On his ship there's alarm, as all rush to see
That young man of the land and the maid of the sea
But an old sailor is wise and covers his ears
Averting his eyes from the sight of her tears

...I am the Siren and this is my song...

That old sailor be praised for breaking her spell
He got the crew moving by sounding the bell
They lowered a boat and rushed out to find
That man who gave his heart and lost his mind

...I am the Siren and this is my song...

When they brought him aboard, he still tried to fight free
Still ensnared by the song of the maid of the sea
But that old sailor lashed out, and said with a hiss
My son, you'd have died with the Siren's first kiss

...I am the Siren and this is my song...

So they battened the hatches and went on their way
But the Siren still thinks of them each passing day
For the lives she takes, there's one less now to claim
One tear less to shed and one life that remains

...I am the Siren and this is my song...

About the Author

To learn more about Bianca D'Arc, please visit www.biancadarc.com. Send an email to Bianca at Bianca@biancadarc.com or join her Yahoo! group to join in the fun with other readers as well as Bianca D'Arc! http://groups.yahoo.com/group/BiancaDArc/

Look for these titles

Now Available:

Dragon Knights 1: Maiden Flight
Dragon Knights 2: Border Lair
Dragon Knights 1 & 2: Ladies of the Lair (combined print edition)
Dragon Knights 3: The Ice Dragon
Lords of the Were
Forever Valentine
Resonance Mates 1: Hara's Legacy

Coming Soon:

Sweeter Than Wine
Wings of Change
FireDrake

War is coming for the knights, dragons, and a damsel who is not quite in distress, but finds her heart's desire in the strong men of the Border Lair.

Maiden Flight

© 2006 Bianca D'Arc

First book in the DragonKnights series.

A chance meeting with a young male dragon seals the fate of one adventurous female poacher. The dragon's partner, a ruggedly handsome knight named Gareth, takes one look at the shapely woman and decides to do a little poaching of his own.

Sir Gareth not only seduces her, but falls deeply in love with the girl who is not only unafraid of dragons but also possesses the rare gift to hear their silent speech. He wants her for his mate, but mating with a knight is no simple thing. To accept a knight, a woman must also accept the dragon, the dragon's mate ... and her knight too.

She is at first shocked, then enticed by the lusty life in the Lair. War is in the making and only the knights and dragons have a chance at ending it before it destroys their land and their lives. But there's nothing a knight enjoys more than a noble quest and winning the heart and trust of a maiden is the noblest quest of all.

Warning, this title contains explicit sex and ménage a trois.

Available now in ebook and print from Samhain Publishing.

War has come to the Border Lair, but as enemies become allies — and lovers — hope springs anew for the dragons and their knights.

Border Lair

© 2006 Bianca D'Arc

Second book in the DragonKnights series.

A young widow, Adora raised her daughter by herself, but her girl is married now. Can Adora find a love of her own in the crowded Border Lair? Dare she even try?

Lord Darian Vordekrais is about to turn traitor, giving up his title, his lands, and his home in order to warn the dragons and knights of his treacherous king's evil plan. Will his life be forfeit or is there some way he can make a new life in a foreign land?

Sir Jared lost his wife and child to treachery, but he knows Lord Darian and trusts him. Both men admire the lovely Adora, but Jared's broken heart is frozen in solid ice. Or is it?

As war comes to the border, the knights and dragons of the Border Lair rise to the occasion. New allies rally to their side. Love blossoms and grows even as evil invades the land. The knights and dragons must stand fast against the onslaught, the beautiful woman of royal blood bringing them hope, healing and love.

Warning, this title contains the following: explicit sex, ménage a trois

A wild Northern Ice Dragon and the girl who raised him save the life of a fierce, shapeshifting royal black dragon, only to have him save them in return...with his love.

The Ice Dragon

© 2006 Bianca D'Arc

The third book in the DragonKnights series.

When a royal black dragon falls under enemy fire, only the wild Northern Ice Dragon and his unlikely female rider can save him. Half wild, like the baby Ice Dragon she calls friend, Lana is a rare and powerful dragon healer. She saves the life of the royal black, only to learn this most sacred of dragons is half-man, able to shift from one form to the other at will.

Roland is king of all dragons and humans in his land but he's far from home, mortally wounded, and his only refuge is the incredible woman who has saved his life and her young wild dragon friend. Lana is the purest form of magic to him, heaven to his senses in both dragon and human form. He knows almost from the first moment that he wants her for his very own.

But a warlord plots in the north, seeking to kill the dragons, who protect the northern border, and overrun Roland's peaceful kingdom. Lana and her incredibly skilled Ice Dragon friend are the only ray of hope for the knights and fighting dragons of the Northern Lair. Just as Lana is the only love Roland will ever know. He can reunite her with her lost family, but can he win her heart and make her his queen?

Warning, this title contains the following: explicit sex explained in graphic terms

Available now in ebook from Samhain Publishing.